THE GARGOYLE'S GLADE

THE GARGOYLE'S GLADE

THE GARGOYLE KNIGHTS

BOOK THREE

L. ALEXANDER

The Gargoyle's Glade
The Gargoyle Knights Book Three

ISBN: 978-1-958933-15-2 (Ebook)
ISBN: 978-1-958933-16-9 (Paperback)

Cover Design: Jessica, Enchanting Covers
Interior Design: Stephanie Anderson, Alt 19 Creative
Edited by: Krista Dapkey

ALSO BY L. ALEXANDER

THE DEMON PRINCES SERIES:
The Demon's Deal
The Demon's Discovery
The Demon's Delight

THE GARGOYLE KNIGHTS SERIES:
The Gargoyle's Grace
The Gargoyle's Gift

NOTE:
Suggested reading order matches publication order as the two series intertwine, have an overarching plot thread and recurring characters throughout. However, each book can be read as a standalone as well, each book is a new couple getting their happily ever after.

For the eldest daughters who just wanted something for themselves,
to not have to always be strong and to really be seen.
You deserve the world.
I humbly offer a fictional grumpy gargoyle who will carry you when
the load gets too heavy. <3

And for Meri, of course. XOXO

YOU

feel like

HOME,

and everywhere

I've never been

ALL AT ONCE.

—BUTTERFLIES RISING

AUTHOR'S NOTE

This is not a dark romance, but there are some potentially triggering themes that come up throughout the book. You can find a list of tropes and content warnings below as well as on my website.

Please reach out to me directly for specifics if needed, I'm more than happy to give details, page numbers—whatever helps you best decide if your mental wellbeing and this story are compatible.

Tropes: fated mates, gargoyles and demons, pseudo-medieval European setting, affection through caretaking, magical power discovery, found family, opposites attract

Content: eldest daughter and parentification trauma, parental loss, discussion of sensory issues, mention of injuries and medical treatment, explicit sexual content, reference to Christian-based mythos for angels/demons/ gargoyles

CHAPTER 1
MERRY

"**H**AVE I SAID thank you for telling me about this place yet today?" I teased my friend Hailon as we made our way away from the bustling city market, arms full of her purchases.

"Only once or twice." She smiled broadly.

Hailon and I had known one another all our lives, though our friendship had truly blossomed in the last couple of years. Ravenglen was home to us both, but she'd traveled here to Revalia with her man not all that long ago, and I could see very plainly that coming here had done infinite good for her. They'd mentioned the city to me before leaving Ravenglen behind, providing an invitation I hadn't initially considered accepting. In fact, many hours had been spent debating before I'd decided on leaving my entire life behind. My horse, Jacks, aside of course. He would never have let me—he'd have chased me down on the road, stamped his hooves, and told me off about my audacity. Compared to this sophisticated, thriving city, my hometown seemed incredibly provincial and lacking in every way. I had no regrets about my decision—Revalia had already far surpassed any dreams I could have had about it in the few short weeks I'd been in residence.

"Well, I mean it just as much as I did an hour ago. Maybe more."

"An hour ago, you were eating a muffin the size of a small melon and drinking some of the most decadent hot chocolate I've ever seen."

I closed my eyes, still tasting the velvety drink on my tongue. "My point stands."

Hailon laughed and linked her arm through mine as we made the final turn toward d'Arcan. The main stone building of the magical academy was already majestic, but the tower reaching into the sky with an observatory atop it was an excellent navigational point from anywhere in the city.

I was still reeling in many ways from simply how much I'd learned since my arrival. Back home, magic was a fleeting concept talked about in hushed conversations when it might be of benefit or cursed when it was being blamed for a problem. Here, it was an integral part of life, though still largely a secret to most of the city's residents. D'Arcan was a place those with magical talent could go to learn about their gifts and other related skills and was run by several members of my friend's new extended family.

"Let's see how Jacks made out with the other horses." Hailon smiled as she opened the iron gate for us at the edge of the collegium's property.

Since our arrival, Jacks and I had been staying with Ophelia, a kind old woman who lived in the forest outside the city gates. Jacks had taken us directly to her house when we'd first arrived, unwilling to change course no matter how hard I'd tried. I'd quickly learned that she was far more than an old woman who liked her privacy. Indeed, Ophelia was a stone kin sorceress. My horse seemed reluctant to leave her hut, but I was feeling as though we'd overstayed our welcome despite assurances from her she didn't mind our company. The last thing I wanted was to abuse her hospitality, and I was ready to move along—I just wasn't sure where I was moving along *to* yet.

We walked through the courtyard and past the main building as well as a small section of garden. Off to one side of the campus, a large section of forested land had been cordoned off. There were wide swaths where the trees had been cut down and construction of several new structures was well underway; the division between the existing grounds and the new stark. The air smelled familiar, like freshly turned earth, but unlike back home, it wasn't because it was planting or harvest season.

There were two girls playing near the horse paddock, chasing one another with little wooden swords while a pair of men who could not have been more opposite from one another watched on, occasionally giving instruction.

"Sara, mind your elbow," Vassago, the one with white hair and silver clothing, said.

"Jana, don't be afraid to strike upward. She's taller, but that doesn't mean she's always got the advantage," the one with dark clothes and black hair added. His name was Rylan, and he was the headmaster of the school. "Ladies, welcome back." The corner of his mouth tilted in a gentle smile. He inclined his head as we approached in greeting.

"Did Jacks behave himself?" I asked, unable to keep myself from smiling as I watched the girls smack their swords together and shout "Ya!" over and over until they collapsed into giggles.

"He was a perfect gentleman," Vassago assured me.

Having spotted me, Jacks ambled over, snorting amicably as he approached the split rail fencing. The other two beasts paid us no attention, too consumed by their grazing.

"Glad to hear it," I replied as I scratched my horse's nose. "I very much appreciate you offering to stable him. I'll admit I hadn't quite thought all the details through when I decided to come here." That was an understatement. I'd left home with only Jacks, a few clothes, a regrettably light purse, and the hope of a fresh start.

"It's our pleasure." Rylan's eyes turned briefly to the sky, where a large black-feathered owl and a raven chattered and played on the breeze. "The other horses could use some company, and there are plenty of empty stalls besides." He turned away from me and waved a hand. "That's enough for today, girls. Bring us your weapons, please."

"Awww," they whined. "Can't we keep them in our room?"

"We could practice after we're done with our schoolwork and chores if we had them in our room!" The younger one turned on every bit of charm she had in her adorable little face.

I exchanged a look with Hailon. Her mouth was quirked into an amused smile. She'd been an only child, but I'd heard that same tone day in and day out with my younger siblings.

"You'll have to discuss that with your sisters," Rylan said, hand held out for his student's sword. "Until then, practice blades stay in the stable if you please."

"But they'll say no!" the older girl protested, a mighty frown on her face.

"Can't imagine why," Vassago muttered with a smirk.

"Then the answer is no, I'm afraid. At least for now. Perhaps when you no longer share, hmm? Stella will be getting her own apartment soon, and Bridget won't be far behind." Rylan patted the girl on her head and gestured toward the main building. "Go on, I'm sure Grace is waiting for you by now. Be sure to tell her it's our fault you're late."

"She doesn't say naughty things as much when we do that." The younger girl nodded sagely, her serious expression forcing me to hold in a laugh.

"Precisely." Rylan winked at the girl and they took off running, giggles floating on the wind.

"They're sweet," I said with a sigh as images of my sisters and brother danced across my mind.

"I'm sure you miss them." Hailon patted the hand I'd left resting on the fence. Jacks, bored with us, as we had no treats, wandered back toward the other horses, tail flicking as he went. At least he was settled in well, that was one less worry on my end.

"Yes." A lump formed in my throat. "So silly. I spent my whole life trying to get away from my bratty, needy siblings, and now I miss all the whining. Their sticky hands. Someone always tugging on my skirt. Makes no sense." A large cat approached and wound its way between my ankles, rubbing its cheeks against my legs. "Hello, there. Aren't you friendly." I reached down to give its head a scratch. I could have sworn when it slowly blinked up at me, I heard a voice say hello back, which was disconcerting but foolish. The creature purred at me for a moment before trotting off into the grass.

I glanced up to see the brothers exchange an amused look.

"No, that makes perfect sense," Hailon assured me, giving my hand another squeeze.

"Indeed," Rylan agreed. He and Vassago stood to the side, watching us. For such large figures, I didn't find them intimidating. It probably helped that I'd first met them with their wives, and literally everyone had been so welcoming it was hard to see them as anything other than kind.

"Shall we apologize to Grace ourselves?" Vassago asked. "She'll likely bless us with tea and snacks if we do."

"I'll never refuse Grace's snacks." Hailon linked her arm in mine again, enthusiasm shining in her eyes.

"Nor would she let you," Rylan chuckled.

My friend looked healthy, happy. Like she'd truly found herself here. It was so different to how she'd been in Ravenglen. My chest squeezed tight with the hope of doing the same for myself.

The stone school building was cool inside, the difference in temperature abrupt from the moment we crossed over the threshold. The late afternoon sun had been keeping me plenty warm, but I suppressed a shiver as we walked down the main hallway and through a wide set of doors.

The expansive dining room made me pause to take a deep breath. Just standing there made my mouth water, the scents coming from the kitchen promising a delicious meal. It was hard to pin down why, especially given the size of it, but the whole space felt like the best parts of coming home after a long day.

The tension in my shoulders eased as the others spoke to one another around me, and I took in the details of the room. Each of the stout wooden posts had a different animal carved into it. The massive hearths at either side of the room kept it the perfect temperature, and I could almost hear the echoes of the students talking as we passed long rows of tables and benches.

"Why's our table clear over there?" Vassago asked. I turned to find him frowning, pointing to a round table and chairs shoved off to the furthest corner of the room.

Grace, a force of a woman who reminded me of my mother in many ways, burst from the kitchen door as though she'd sensed our presence. I'd met her twice already, and both times the energy about her was exactly the same.

"Ah! Yes, there you two are. The little helpers you finally returned to me for their chores are assembling your tea. Care to lend a hand?" Without waiting for a response, she quickly vanished again out the doorway we'd just entered through.

Rylan and Vassago looked at one another curiously, then followed her out.

"Should we ..." I started, but Hailon shook her head.

"No, I'm sure they've got it. Grace would have given us a task. I've learned it's best to stay out of her way unless she specifically asks."

Moments later, the men reappeared along with two others, a giant upside-down table and several chairs carried between them. I blinked and my face grew hot as I took in the familiar broad forms. One was Coltor, a stone kin man I'd met at Ophelia's house shortly after I'd arrived in Revalia.

He was Hailon's friend, and I couldn't seem to avoid seeing him no matter where I went in this expansive city. His father, Magnus, was likely the other set of broad shoulders under the huge slab of wood they were carrying. Grace directed them tidily around corners and between benches, and Hailon and I scuttled out of the way as the table was flipped legs down and set near where we'd been standing. We collected the chairs from the round table and slid them into the empty spots around the new large rectangular one.

Grace stood back once everything was settled where she wanted it, a pleased smile on her face. She pulled a rag from her apron pocket and polished a spot on the wood to a glossy shine. "I'll miss the old one," she gestured vaguely to the round one in the corner, "but this one has plenty of room to grow." Her twinkling eyes grazed mine as she turned, and Magnus tucked her under his arm, pressing a kiss to her hair as they went into the kitchen.

Rylan smiled as he ran one finger along the surface. "Calla will be pleased. I wasn't sure when she told me which one she'd decided on, but I shouldn't have doubted her."

Vassago chuffed. "We should all know by now not to doubt them, but we can't seem to help ourselves, can we?"

The brothers looked dreamy, gazes far away as they commiserated about their wives. Hailon smothered a laugh as she looked my way. She was fooling herself though; I'd met her man, and he was their brother. He was just as besotted with her.

"Well, I'll be on my way." Coltor glanced at me, then turned to leave as Grace and Magnus returned, arms full of plates and cups.

"You will not. Sit." Magnus grinned at his son, the expression on his face softening the tone with which the words were delivered.

Grace distributed teacups and started to pour. "Please," she added. "We so rarely see you. Can't you at least stay for some tea?"

Coltor glanced around, discomfort obvious, but he selected a seat. The one directly across from me.

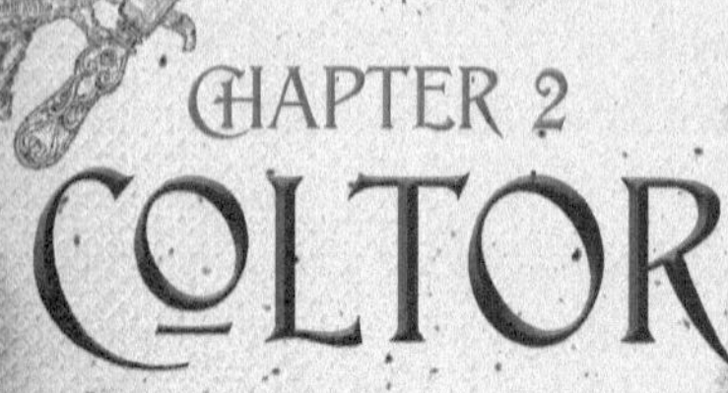

CHAPTER 2
COLTOR

HUTS AND CABINS had sprung up around the ruins like mushrooms after a thorough rain.

Initially, I'd thought it wouldn't be so bad to have a neighbor or two, isolated as the location was, but now I was having second thoughts. In fact, I was curious how we'd arrived at a place where more people inhabiting the area was desirable at all.

The Ruins of Emankor were intentionally magically warded so people avoided coming too close to them. The whole point of my holding a sentry post here was to scare wayward travelers *away*. Now, the ruins were going to be home to several residents, both permanent and temporary. It was too late to dispute the new development however, as the plans had already been approved and construction started.

"Stay to the path," I groused at a handful of young stone kin men carting lumber on their shoulders. They were paying no attention and tramping down the grass and flowers as they crossed the glade.

"Sorry," one of them apologized, and they mindfully returned to the narrow strip of dirt. It had been well traveled recently, and several branches had sprouted off the main one, creating easy routes from the portals through the glade and some all the way to the other side of the ruins.

So many of my clan had been in and out via the portal to Revalia in recent times it had left my head spinning. It had been nice to see others of my kind, but my enthusiasm was very rapidly depleted. I missed the quiet that had plagued me to near madness not all that long ago.

If nothing else, at least my hut remained hidden away. It was tucked right outside the boundary of the ancient castle itself, and was built with just the most basic of comforts in mind. It had, after all, been intended simply to provide shelter while I was posted as sentry here. Nobody could have foreseen then that I might be the only one able to take or maintain the post for months or years at a time. Small as it was, the single little room had served me well over the years. I'd added a few bits of my own after being there for so long, but it remained not much more than a barrack.

The second dwelling had only recently been built. Seir and Hailon's cabin, nestled beyond the tree line in the heart of the glade, was, from the very beginning, a home. They were good neighbors, quiet. Friendly. And thanks to Seir, I was able to step away from my post now and then as he and his brother Tap managed the many doorways between worlds hidden within the ruined bones of the ancient castle that fell under my responsibility.

The pair had fallen into the ruins as they were journeying through. Our friendship had roots in what was purely an accidental meeting, but had developed normally enough. I'd threatened him, he'd stabbed me for speaking too harshly to his mate ... and somehow, they now lived within shouting distance. We'd all become good friends. The first I'd had in quite some time.

Now, my kin were building a whole series of little dwellings, and I was struggling to keep up with the rapid changes. To my dismay, I'd lashed out several times when really what would probably have served me better was some time to quietly process what was happening.

I'd gotten too good at being alone.

Turning from the noisy construction, I made my way to the portal that would take me into Revalia. I'd been summoned by my father to help with an urgent task, and I didn't want to be away any longer than necessary.

MOVING A TABLE. That was my father's idea of an urgent task.

He'd even had help from the two demons who lived at the collegium for which the table was being procured. When I asked why I'd been needed at all, he'd just smiled at me, like he'd won something. It was beyond irritating.

So now I was seated across from Hailon's friend in the dining room of the collegium when I should be back in my glade.

The little woman with hair the color of a summer sunset was somehow everywhere I looked lately. My jaw clenched as my pulse picked up against my will.

Merry. Her sunny disposition was a perfect embodiment of the happy moniker. I was inexorably drawn to bask in her light like a lovesick youngling, and it disturbed me greatly that I couldn't seem to escape such an inclination.

When she'd first popped up at my several-times great-aunt Ophelia's hut, I'd been unable to do much more than blink and stare at her. I'd gone to visit the ancient gargoyle sorceress for help managing a newfound power, one that still felt unwieldy and had me doubting my strength. It had not bolstered my confidence at all that I'd been largely unable to speak in her presence during that introduction. Thankfully, I'd moved beyond stuttered greetings and halting words with her, though admittedly not by much.

Not long after that initial meeting, she'd been here at d'Arcan. I'd used the portal so I could have a quick discussion with my father, and there she was, bold as anything, giving advice on how to expand the garden beds. Rylan, the demon archmage who'd founded the collegium, had enthusiastically gestured and said something that made her clap her hands excitedly. I'd stared from across the yard, watching her laugh freely with the collection of demons, gargoyles, and mages like she'd always been there.

I couldn't even escape her at the markets when I'd gone for supplies. My father's mate, Grace, had taken her to shop, and Merry's bright laugh had me turning around from the opposite end of the street to find the source of the joyous sound.

It didn't seem to matter where I went. That smile, those vibrant red curls, that strange magnetism ... they were everywhere I turned.

And now, she was here. Again. Staring at me across the new dining table over tea.

"Sorry?" I realized I hadn't been paying attention as she looked at me expectantly.

"Sugar?" Her cheeks flushed pink as she pushed the dish of little white cubes toward me.

"No, thank you."

"Are you still staying with Ophelia, Merry?" my father asked her, wearing a frown of concern.

Ophelia was terrifying. Mostly kind, to be sure, but ancient and therefore infinitely dangerous.

"Yes." She bowed her head, stirring the sugar into her tea. "She's been so gracious, but it's time I moved on. I'd love to leave her to her peace and quiet as soon as I can."

"I don't see any reason you can't claim the first guest cabin in the glade. I think all it's missing is paint. You and I could tackle that if there's nobody else to get it done." Hailon brightened, clearly taken with the idea.

"Is she ... prepared for that?" I asked.

"Prepared?" Hailon tilted her head in confusion. "As prepared as I was, you mean?" Her eyebrow raised. She never hesitated to ask questions that had me biting back knee-jerk responses. I appreciated and was frustrated by that in equal measure.

"Yes. Something like that." If she wasn't, we'd all have to manage the inevitable consequences of having to educate her about a great number of alarming things.

"We've discussed plenty," Hailon confirmed.

"I'm sure she's trustworthy. You should know that well enough as she's been staying with Ophelia all this time." My father's words rolled over me as he sat back in his chair, gaze heavy. I couldn't help the ingrained flash of shame that came as he crossed his arms over his chest. It was the pose he used either when he was gearing up for a lecture or disappointed in one of us. "You've managed your post well all this time on your own, son. I can understand why you'd be possessive of it."

"I'm not *possessive*," I argued, anger rising quickly in my blood, "but there are reasons it's guarded from outsiders. Or have you forgotten?"

My father grew serious and affirmed that he did indeed remember, which assuaged the heat in my veins.

Merry's cheeks were rosy with embarrassment as she glanced between the faces at the table, clearly unsure what she'd gotten herself in the middle of.

"We live there too, now," Hailon put in, quickly turning a smile on me. "And there will be others, sooner or later. We can all help her understand if there's something she needs to learn. She's taken quite well to all I've explained to her already." Hailon raised an eyebrow, conveying very clearly she'd been busy getting her friend educated about the unique residents of this city and beyond. "Besides, another set of eyes is always good, right? If strangers wander through, there's someone else to raise the alarm. Think of it, between us and her for neighbors, you'll likely never be hungry or bored ever again." Her multicolor eyes danced with mirth.

I glanced from the pair of friends to the demons and even my father, who all sat grinning quietly, like they knew a secret. Or perhaps like this was all well planned, and I was simply the last to find out.

Merry's mouth opened, but it took a moment for her to find her voice. Her deep-brown eyes held mine from across the table. "It's okay to say no. I can continue staying with Ophelia. She told me it was fine, I just—"

"You're also welcome to a room here at d'Arcan, Merry. We've a spare staff apartment available," Rylan offered.

"Thank you, that's very generous." She swallowed before continuing. "I'm not above sleeping on a sofa if it came to that. Goodness knows I survived far worse back home. There were more of us than there were beds." She gave a short, self-deprecating laugh and started nervously braiding a little section of her hair. "I've never had a place to myself, though. I'll admit there is a certain appeal to that." Merry's blush deepened, turning her whole face and even the upper part of her chest pink. I tensed, the color strangely tantalizing. "What I mean to say is, there are plenty of alternatives if this arrangement isn't going to work for you."

My breath stalled, and I fought a rising wave of frustration. I would look cruel if I didn't say yes. But I couldn't blame them for that, not really. Yes, I was annoyed, but mostly I was nervous. Until very recently, I'd spent a whole lot of time alone. Socializing was difficult at best. Being in close proximity with a woman that tied both my tongue and chest in knots was going to be a challenge. I inhaled slowly through my nose, willing my thoughts to settle.

"I'll explain anything that comes up," Hailon promised. "And we'll be here most days, besides. You probably won't see her any more than you see us."

That was likely true. I was out in the ruins most nights on patrol and either rested or stone slept during the day. The completed cabin not far from my hut had a furnished bedroom available whereas Hailon and Seir only had a sofa to offer. It did make sense, even if it was the most terrifying option.

"I suppose that would be fine."

"Perfect," Hailon said, clapping her hands together and breaking the tension that had formed. "Thank you, Coltor."

Merry turned grateful eyes my way, one of her hands resting briefly over the fingers I was gripping the little teacup handle with. She gestured for me to lean forward and when I did, she stood and leaned over the table. Confused, I just sat there, blinded by her smile as she planted a light kiss on my cheek. "Thank you very much. You'll hardly know I'm there."

That was impossible.

Lightning flashed through my veins in response to her touch and my heart squeezed like it had been gripped by a fist as visions went off behind my eyes.

The conversation resumed around us, but I could only stare at her. The blood drained from my face, nausea tangling in my gut.

Thankfully, she didn't seem to notice, as she'd turned sideways to discuss something with Hailon as they piled Grace's honey cakes and fruit onto their plates.

I'd learned plenty about Merry in the short time since her arrival. She was sunshine incarnate, with a mind—and tongue, if so prompted—as sharp as my best blade. She was organized, efficient. As far as I could tell, she was good with children and animals. To my vexation, she was also beautiful beyond all reasonable measure. All of this made her a potential weakness, one I hadn't been expecting and wasn't at all prepared for.

And when she'd touched me, I'd seen a glimpse of her future, just as I had when I'd shaken her hand when we first met.

Except this time, in the future I saw, Merry would soon be dead.

CHAPTER 3
MERRY

HALLON BOUNCED FROM market stall to market stall, asking me my opinion on towels, linens, countertop baskets that were pretty but wouldn't serve any decent functionality at all. It was funny to me, because the day I'd arrived in Revalia, she'd dragged me to this very spot so she could pick out some things for herself, and she hadn't shown half the enthusiasm.

"I don't have money for any of this," I laughed. "I'm not sure why we're even here."

"I'm trying to find some things for your cabin," she chided. "Maybe a housewarming gift. But you're not making it very easy."

I shook my head and waved away the two different patterns of stoneware plates a merchant offered to me. "It's not mine though, and I don't need a gift. If anything, I feel like Coltor needs one. Did you see his face?"

"What about his face?" she prodded.

"He was about to break some teeth he had his jaw clenched so hard."

"Strong jawline, yes."

"Stop." I laughed at my friend's obvious attempt at playful matchmaking. "He was frowning so much he basically only had one eyebrow."

"That can be fixed with some grooming though."

"For the love ... Yes, I noticed that he's *handsome*. Is that what you're trying to get at? But I don't think he likes anyone much, let alone me. I'm a fresh nuisance he has to deal with. He doesn't seem at all pleased to be getting another neighbor."

Hailon sighed, hands on her hips and a gentle smile on her mouth. "I think he might surprise you. At least, I hope he will. And that land isn't actually his, though we do all kind of act that way. He's just been out there the longest." She sighed and turned away from the stalls. "Blue or green?"

"What?"

"Blue. Or. Green?"

"Green?"

"White or yellow?"

"What exactly are we talking about?" I laughed, amused by her high spirits if nothing else. I'd nearly never seen her this excitable back in Ravenglen.

"Paint. White or yellow?"

"Yellow, I suppose. But it has to be the right shade."

"Exactly right. Come on, I have an idea."

It was quite some time later that we finally made it back to Ophelia's hut carrying a rolled-up canvas swatched with several different colors of yellow and their complementary greens, along with a bag of odds and ends she'd refused to leave the market without. Hailon flinched at the edge of Ophelia's property, but I was not bothered by the warding like she was. That was a mystery everyone who'd noticed had been trying to figure out since I'd arrived.

The door opened as we approached, the stout old woman smiling wide as she greeted us.

"Your timing is good girls, I've just pulled the bread out of the oven. Come in, come in."

We followed her into her cozy little home, and I excused myself to pack up the last of my meager belongings from the small guest bedroom before joining them in the living room.

Ophelia doled out delicate little teacups, the contents of which were mostly whiskey with the barest splash of tea. The bread was sliced and steaming on a tray alongside little pots of honey and butter.

"I truly have enjoyed our time together, Merry," Ophelia said, seeing my bags. "I hope you're not leaving on my account." She tipped the cup to her lips and finished it in a single go.

"Not at all," I insisted. "I appreciate your hospitality very much. A cabin near Hailon was recently finished and Coltor offered it to me." That was an embellishment, for sure, but close enough. "I couldn't refuse a temptation like that. I've never lived on my own."

"How wonderful to be young and eager for new experiences." Ophelia chuckled. The moment was interrupted by a sudden and insistent tapping. "Expecting someone?" she asked us earnestly.

"No, not at all," Hailon answered. "Besides, I'm pretty sure that was coming from the window, not the door."

With a grunt, the ancient gargoyle got to her feet and crossed to a stained-glass window behind a table covered in an assortment of small items. She'd rearranged the things atop it several times since I'd arrived, adding different crystals, a book, salt. I hadn't managed to puzzle out the meaning of it, but I didn't need to—sorceress work was well beyond my understanding. Before coming to Revalia, I'd been a simple store clerk and cleaner after all.

Ophelia swung the colorful pane open and stepped back. A small owl with big yellow eyes flapped into view, settling on the sill. "Hello there. Aren't you charming! Have we met?" Ophelia addressed the creature.

I froze in place as those golden eyes locked onto mine. Hailon spoke to me, and I stiffened. I could see her lips moving, but could not hear her voice. My heart pounded painfully in my chest and my breath was stifled to sharp pants. Ophelia turned as well, all eyes suddenly and heavily resting on me.

Friend? The voice was quiet, barely more than a muffled whisper in my mind. My whole body flinched. I went hot, then cold as it happened again. *Friend, help? Bond?*

"Do you hear that?" I asked Hailon, a tremor in my voice.

"Hear what?" she frowned at me.

Ophelia, on the other hand, exclaimed happily. The bird startled at the sudden rough noise, wings out and clawed feet tapping on the wooden window sill. "Sorry, sorry." She patted the bird on the head in apology, then turned back to me, a pleased look on her face. "That explains quite a lot, actually."

"You can hear it?" I forced the words from my throat, muscles aching from how tightly strung they'd become.

She nodded, fingers gently petting the feathers between the bird's eyes. "Easy now. Gentle." The golden orbs closed, shielded by the bird's inner lids, and I could move again. "You and Calla should have a talk. Have you met her cat?"

"Cat?"

"Or the birds? There are several familiars at d'Arcan now. They all live there quite harmoniously."

"Familiars?" I knew I sounded foolish, but the single words were all I could manage as I tried to sort out what was happening.

"Whose is that?" Hailon asked, amused by the petite bird.

It turned its head in that decidedly unsettling way owls had, and looked directly at Ophelia.

"Oh, I see. Well. I'll send a message to the demon in charge of things then, if requests are getting backed up that badly. I'll take care of it, don't you worry."

I had learned plenty since my arrival, but I found myself as lost as I'd felt the first day when Hailon had informed me that her charming man was a demon and her in-laws as well. Their friends were stone kin—gargoyles—and she was a null, someone who could cancel out magic. It boggled my mind, but honestly it also made a certain kind of sense. I'd yet to figure out why any of that actually mattered, however. They were all lovely, kind people, and she was the same woman I knew from back home.

"Can someone please explain why I can hear the bird speaking to me in my head? And why it felt like I was paralyzed when it looked at me?"

Ophelia patted the bird again, and it flew off. She closed the window and refilled her cup of whiskey tea before taking a seat.

"First things first. What did our charming little friend say to you?" she asked me, reaching for two thick slices of bread and the pot of honey. She handed me one, keeping the other for herself. "Eat that, the sugar will help."

I did as she instructed, having to chase the thick honey with my tea. If nothing else, at least the whiskey loosened my throat again. "I think it asked for help? Something about a bond?" I finally managed.

Ophelia chuckled as she chewed, head bobbing enthusiastically. "Yes, yes. Well, isn't that wonderful! Now they'll have someone other than me to go to. The immobilization should get better with some practice. Seems he was rather eager to get his message across and perhaps was a bit heavy-handed to be sure he could communicate with you. We can probably find you a trinket or stone to help with that."

My mind spun, none of the thoughts coming through in a comprehensive way. "I don't understand."

"Familiars, like that little owl, speak mainly to their bonded. They tend to keep it within the family, in a way—mages, witches, fae, and the like. But there are outliers like myself who can communicate with all of them as a kind of ..." She waved her hand, searching for the right word. "Intermediary. A conduit. Seems you're like me in that way."

"How? Why?"

"That's the mystery, now isn't it?" She smiled. "It used to be that the crossroads demon managed all the paperwork and there was a stone kin or witch assigned as Keeper to manage all the creatures topside. They'd offer blessings, hear grievances. Negotiate population sizes and needs for their area, things like that. The animals all had an emissary of sorts too, so they could check in periodically, offer their support to the Keeper if needed. It was a very symbiotic relationship and ensured the health of nature as a whole." She pursed her lips thoughtfully. "But there hasn't been a Keeper in ages, not since ... Well, I'm not even sure, it's been so long." Ophelia pulled at a chin whisker while she pondered, eyes squinted as she sifted through her memories. "No matter. The absence of a Keeper is likely why the ability to hear them has started cropping up more in individuals like yourself. Spread out the duty, help the balance."

Ophelia tilted her head, eyes narrowed. "Come sit." She patted the cushion to her right and set her cup on the low table in front of her. "As far as I can tell, you're not stone kin. But that doesn't mean you're strictly human either."

I did as she asked, and the old woman took my face in her warm hands once I was seated, intelligent eyes searching mine. After a thorough inspection, she took my hands in hers, tracing the lines in my palms and the blue veins in my wrists. Thoughtful noises rolled from her throat. She paused, examining my bracelet. Her finger turned the small stone woven into the center around. "Red jasper? That's an interesting choice."

"My father hunted stones. It was one of his favorite hobbies. He brought several of these home one season when he was helping dig new wells. He said the color reminded him of me." I touched my hair.

"Yes, yes. I can understand that. Is this your work?"

"No, I've no talent for this kind of thing. The bracelet has been in my family for ages. There are strands of hair in the braid of the band from everyone who's worn it since my many-times great-grandmother on my father's side. My mother added the stone and it became mine after ..." I swallowed, the old pain somehow still had a sting in it. "After he left." He'd gone on a trip to hunt for precious stones, perhaps gold. There'd been a disastrous collapse in the old mine he was thought to be in. Nothing had ever been the same again.

Ophelia patted my hand sympathetically and moved on with her inspection, still humming.

"Merry's family has been in Ravenglen for at least five generations," Hailon said helpfully. "I know that guarantees nothing, but the odds of her being human are fairly high."

Ophelia looked away from me to Hailon for a brief second, amusement putting a twinkle in her eye. "Says the girl with a mix of all six factions in her blood who knew very little about herself until not all that long ago."

Hailon was chagrined, but she smiled. "Well, that's *me*, not her."

"Yes, yes. But you were a very welcome guest here with me as well, with just as many of your own mysteries. That much is true." The examination continued, with Ophelia tracing the dimensions of my ears and counting the little bumps of bone down my upper spine. She frowned, then got to her feet, pulling me by the hand to follow her.

She took me over to the table of mysterious items and started rearranging them all again.

"Finger?" she asked. Confused, I offered my hand and she pricked my index finger, then squeezed a drop of blood into the tiny iron cauldron.

"What's that for?" I asked, pushing the pad of my thumb against the tiny spot of blood to ease the sting away.

"Information." Ophelia's hands moved surprisingly fast as she shifted things around.

A piece of rose quartz got relocated from the right side of the table to the left, and a small obelisk of obsidian was removed altogether. Salt and some kind of grain went into the cauldron with some dried wood shavings like the kind we used in the stables back home. The candle underneath suddenly had a flame, though I hadn't seen her strike a flint.

Smoke rose in a slow gray curl, and Hailon's hand clasped mine. Her brief smile was meant to be reassuring, but I could feel her tension.

The smoke formed what looked like words as it traveled higher in the air. Ophelia muttered to herself, the tendrils shifting and reforming in a way that shouldn't have been possible.

"That's not what happened for me." Hailon's voice was low, but she seemed relieved.

"This is different. Merry is different," Ophelia said in response, arm raised as she traced along the curly swirls with a fingertip, careful not to actually touch or disturb them as she puzzled out their meaning.

"What happened for you?" I asked.

"I saw faces. My parents."

"Oh." I squeezed her arm. That was beyond significant for Hailon considering she'd been raised by her mother's friend, a woman Hailon knew as Aunt Sal, since she was very small. She had never actually known her parents.

As the smoke began to falter and dissipate, Ophelia moved as quickly as she was able to get a quill and a journal. Hastily, she sketched down what she'd seen. "Better than nothing," she muttered, then she threw the window open again so the smoke would clear. "Human," she nodded. "Though there must be something magical in there allowing this talent to bloom. Likely a hedge witch, somewhere back in the line. Perhaps some other kind of mage." Ophelia patted my shoulder and her eyes crinkled. "You're a rare find, Merry. Seems you belong here with us."

My face grew hot. Hearing that kind of sentiment delivered so casually was far more potent than I could have expected. I missed my family dearly, but I'd left to find something more for myself and somehow ... I'd already found it.

"Mostly it's been demons bringing me fascinating women, but I suppose in this case I've got a horse to thank," Ophelia sighed, making short work of her abandoned tea and pouring another.

"Wait, is Jacks ...?" He'd never tried to speak in my mind that I could recall, but I was discounting nothing at this point.

"He's definitely something special. Don't fret over it, though. If he can and wants to, he will. What's meant to be will be." The ancient sorceress turned and started to hunt along her bookshelves for something. She plucked a thin volume out, one bound in rich tan leather. "Take this. It should help."

"Thank you."

She settled back into her chair with a groan. "You'll be coming to see me soon, I'll wager. The invitation is standing, mind. My door is always open to you. Both of you."

"Thank you," I repeated, feeling numb.

"You're the same as you always were, Merry, despite this new knowledge." Ophelia patted my hand. "You're still quite human, just one with an ancestor that passed along a very unique gift." Her brow wrinkled. "That gift may be heavy at times, simply because the threads of magic in your blood are few. Not weak, understand, just not dominant and not well trained. Present enough to produce your gift, but perhaps not enough to adequately support it without help." She frowned, then was suddenly on her feet again, leaving my head spinning even more than it had been. "Your escort is here."

I glanced at Hailon, silently asking how she knew someone had arrived when there'd been no sound at all. My friend just shook her head.

And then I froze again, because not only was Hailon's man, Seir, outside, so was Coltor.

CHAPTER 4
COLTOR

"SO WHAT?" OPHELIA asked, an infuriatingly calm expression on her face.

Seir and Hailon had taken Merry back with them to the glade already. I'd thought I would be joining them, but my elder had interrupted those plans.

"How do I explain that to her?"

"You just say it. Use your words, Coltor. It's not as difficult as you're making it."

My mouth dropped open, and I stumbled over several false starts before I could commit to speaking again. "How do I begin such a conversation? 'Hello, Merry, apologies for ruining your day, but I had a mysterious vision when you touched me, and in it you were dead. Sorry about that.'"

Ophelia snorted in amusement. "Perhaps a bit more demurely, sure. She's new to some of the parts of this world, Coltor, not incompetent. In fact—"

My volume increased, a frustrated noise rumbling out of my throat. "That's *not* what I mean." I caught myself, but too late. I'd interrupted my elder and *growled* at her. That alone could have ended my existence. Thankfully, she looked more amused by my outburst and lack of manners than murderous. "Apologies, Ophelia. I mean no offense. But she ... she didn't ask for any of this. And according to my vision, she's going to *die*. That feels very urgent."

The old woman, still grinning, grunted and waved a hand at me as though I were the one being ridiculous. "Of course she will, nephew. Like it or not, none of us escape that particular fate. No matter how long it might take to get there." Her smile faded, and her gaze took on a faraway quality. The shift in the energy within her little hut had my skin crawling.

"Of course. But what I mean is, she will die *soon*. Perhaps only days from now, it's hard to know for sure." Unease slithered through my stomach again, the terrifying flash of future I'd gotten over tea at d'Arcan replaying behind my eyes. The thought of that vibrant woman suddenly ceasing to exist was more than I could stomach.

"She *might*. And you know as well as I do that time is relative." She shook her head and I felt like a child being scolded as she turned a disappointed look on me. "You're giving this new gift too much control, Coltor. It's showing you possibilities, not absolutes. It is fully within your power to direct how things go."

"It's always the worst outcome that comes true though."

I'd only had a handful of visions, but they'd all skewed to the most negative scenario when they'd come to pass. The old merchant who'd injured himself trying to keep fruit from spilling off his cart because of a clumsy child. The discovery that the milled grain in one of the warehouses was tainted with toxic mold after a whole section of the city grew ill and Hailon went to help heal them. The reason for rats congregating in a drainage ditch being the body of a missing man.

"Always?" She scoffed. "I believe that may be an exaggeration. And your experience pool isn't very reliable, now is it?"

She wasn't wrong. I rolled my shoulders back, trying to release some of the tension. "Perhaps. But I don't want it to go that way."

"So change it. Change the visions. Forsee more possibilities so that you can tip the scales in a fairer direction. If I were a betting woman, I'd wager that the outcome is more even than you think."

I tilted my head and stared, molars grinding together. I knew she wasn't being intentionally flippant, but her tone was infuriating. "Do you have a suggestion for how I might go about such a thing?" The diplomatic words scraped out of my throat. "I've no clue how to incite visions at will."

"It's not *my* gift, nephew. That is for you to work out. I've already given you what help I can."

Her lack of insight and my own feeling of helplessness only exacerbated the frustration bubbling in my veins.

"I was perfectly happy minding my own business until that demon stumbled into the ruins. Seir showing up was one of the first bad endings I was shown." I'd foreseen that a demon would come into the ruins and we'd battle. Seir was indeed a demon, and we had fought. I'd even taken injury from his blade. But I'd been deserving of his wrath in that moment, and as far as demons went ... he wasn't so bad.

Ophelia laughed then, full and heartily. It went on so long tears started running down her cheeks. "Is that what you believe? Truly? That Seir and Hailon interrupting your tragically boring existence at that post in the ruins was a bad thing? That Merry showing up here with that horse like she did is something negative?" She laughed loud and openly, her shoulders shaking and hand slapping along the arm of her chair.

I stared back at her and all the bluster left my body. My chin dropped to my chest, and I scrubbed at my face with my hands, willing some sanity to return to me. "No." Their friendship had proven something I desperately needed, and Merry arriving was many things, but none of them bad.

"No, indeed. Good lad." She patted my knee as though I were still a youngling who admitted to filching a sweet from the kitchen. "You were lonely, whether you want to admit it or not. And you were unwittingly slipping into the beginning stages of all the wonderful types of madness that tend to plague our kind when we focus too much on our duty and not enough on our souls." Such profound knowledge and wisdom always came from her mouth so casually, like it was the simplest thing in the world.

Seir's close proximity and talent had allowed me to get away from my post. Hailon's easily offered friendship had reminded me that not everyone was a threat. They were good neighbors. And one could very much argue that Hailon's mere presence had drawn Merry, who was something else entirely.

"Perhaps."

"Not perhaps. I know you're young yet, but you were on the verge of something destructive, Coltor. Trust me, I know the signs."

This assertion and the way she blinked slowly, like she was battling her own memories, only furthered the itchy tingle that had settled under my skin. "Do you get lonely out here by yourself, Ophelia?"

She gave a dry laugh, but I could see the flicker of sorrow under her smile. "I'm quite used to being alone, and in many ways prefer it. Loneliness and I are old companions. I thought ..." She paused, stopping long enough to pour herself a fresh cup of whiskey tea, lingering so long between the halves of her sentence I began to wonder if she'd abandoned it altogether. When her voice came again, it was low, and I knew it would be best to stay away at least a few days. I'd acted out, then asked the wrong questions of my elder, and her mood had turned dark. More salted licorice from the city would certainly be required for me to return. "After my sister and I had our ... falling out, she returned to the conclave permanently and I remained here in the Dread Forest, safe under my wards." Her eyes met mine, a soft sheen in them. "She's well?"

"As far as I know, yes."

Ophelia's sister, Euphemia, was centuries younger than her, and thrived on theatrics. In fact, she was the voice of the conclave and hosted all the celebrations. How the pair of them had gotten along at all was a mystery to most of us, as were the details of the fight that had separated them.

"Good, good." She gazed off again briefly, then collected herself and returned to the conversation. "I'll likely stay here, alone, until the time comes for me to return to the stones. That's what I signed up for when I denied things like my mate bond and a council seat, after all. A quiet existence, very few visitors. No ... entanglements. The city and other stone kin are close enough, should I require something. In some ways, this is much like what you had, until recently, yes?"

I went with the only response I felt was neutral enough to be safe. There were several nuggets of profound information in what she'd said to me, things that certainly weren't common knowledge if they were known to anyone at all. "Yes ma'am."

"But I was incorrect in my calculations. I was not yet finished helping others or taking on students." A weak grin returned, a flicker of the friendly light returning to her eyes. She suddenly appeared very tired and worry replaced my fear. "The fates are constantly balancing, Coltor. That's why you sometimes see multiple outcomes. All are possible, depending on what steps you choose along the way. You just have to choose wisely."

"How do I do that?"

She shook her head. "I don't know. But I can't conceive of any circumstance where there wouldn't be more than one possible outcome, even if you are only *shown* one."

I scrubbed a hand over my face, more vexed than I'd been when I arrived. "I need more time to figure this gift out properly. This is too much, too fast."

The corner of her mouth lifted. "You don't have that luxury, nephew." Her head tilted as she sipped from her ridiculously delicate little teacup, watching me closely. "When did the visions start? I know you came to me not long after you began having them, but do you have any idea what the catalyst was?"

"It started not long after an elixir was doled out to all stone kin soldiers."

"Elixir?"

"Remembrance."

"Oh? I haven't heard about that one. I assume it was Greta that made it for you?"

"Yes, she did." Greta was a stone kin who had a particularly strong talent with alchemy. She was also the wife of one of the demons who lived at d'Arcan and a cousin of mine who'd been hidden away from us much of her life.

"And what exactly were all the soldiers being asked to remember?"

"My father and General Gaius are working on something to do with the council. Everyone was made to take the elixir to be sure they weren't forgetting important events. To find out whether or not something we'd been given by our command had stolen our memories."

"And?"

I shook my head. "I was one of the lucky ones. I wasn't missing many, and nothing vital. A few days after they were restored, the visions started."

"Mmm." She made a thoughtful noise in her throat. "So whatever you were given to remove those memories may have been suppressing this gift."

That was the logical conclusion I'd come to myself. I hadn't shared it with anyone else yet, however. "Yes."

"Better late than never. Though gifts can come on a bit strong if held back unnaturally. I'm certain you'll manage it well, in any case." Her tone was resolute; the subject now closed.

I got to my feet, understanding her cue. "I should be on my way."

"You're welcome back here anytime you need my help, nephew. Your invitation is open, as is my door."

"I appreciate that." And I did, but I would not be abusing the privilege. I would be returning with candy and one of her other more favored students. Perhaps one of my sisters or Hailon could accompany me when I came to visit next.

Ophelia's gait was stiff as she led the way slowly from her cozy living room through the little kitchen. It took perhaps ten of my steps to thirty of hers. As she opened the heavy wooden door she seemed out of sorts, far more than I'd seen her since I first started to visit.

"Can I get you anything before I go, Ophelia?"

Her eyes roved the front yard, woodland creatures scattering at our presence. "No, no. I'm going to have a bite to eat, perhaps some more tea, and then take a rest. You go on." I ducked down to kiss her cheek, and she patted my shoulder. "You're a good lad. So much like your father. Your mother too. She's where you get your iron will, you know. Ygritte was special, and your gifts are similar, whether they seem so or not." I blinked, flattered by the comparison. It was rare that anyone spoke of my mother, and Ophelia's easy mention of her warmed me. "Things will work out, Coltor, but not without some effort. Discomfort, too. Let your big, kind heart guide you. Many things will become clear soon enough." She grinned again and chuckled, leaving me feeling all the more like I'd missed something important.

"Yes ma'am. Thank you." I inhaled before I stepped out the door, knowing her wards were going to press in on me. The sensations of fear and panic had become familiar, but were no less disconcerting now than they had been weeks ago.

"I'll see you soon, nephew." Ophelia didn't wait for me to start walking away, she just shut the door.

My stomach rolled, anxiety from the intense wards mixing with my concern for her. Her eyes had grown increasingly vacant throughout our conversation, and it seemed her body was beginning to follow suit. I'd never seen her violent, but hollow seemed as bad. Worse, perhaps.

I deployed my wings and flew back into Revalia to d'Arcan so I could utilize the portal. I didn't stop to greet anyone, too anxious about returning to my post. I'd already been gone far longer than I'd intended, and I didn't want to risk having to explain to anyone why I was lost in my thoughts.

CHAPTER 5
MERRY

"I AM ..." I STOPPED to take some slow breaths, willing the contents of my stomach to settle back where they belonged. "Still very unsure about portals."

"Hailon felt just the same. It'll get better!" Seir, who was perpetually happy, patted my shoulder and started off down the path toward the cabin I'd be borrowing with my belongings.

I'd visited the glade once before, in Hailon's effort to help me understand the breadth of new knowledge I'd stumbled into by coming to Revalia. As with that time, the sensation of the portal was uncomfortable at best.

"What helped you?" I asked her when my insides had stopped spinning enough to walk. I turned my bracelet around my wrist, the idle gesture comforting.

The air was warmer here, more humid. Immediately I started musing over what plants I might be able to cultivate in such a place.

Hailon shrugged before handing the paint-swatched canvas over to me. "Time, mostly. Plenty of trips back and forth—it really does get better every time, I promise. Reminding myself how incredibly handy they are helped too."

"Don't forget being carried!" Seir yelled from several long paces ahead.

Hailon sighed. "That part didn't hurt, I suppose." He was looking over his shoulder and smiled at her capitulation. The demon had three sharp canines instead of one, but his grin didn't strike me as threatening.

"Well, unfortunately, I don't have anyone to carry me," I teased.

Seir chuckled loudly to himself. "Yet."

"He's a bit ..."

"Odd, yes." Hailon nodded, but her soft smile told me she loved him all the same. "He means well, though. And you're lovely, Merry, if you want to find someone to carry you, it won't take much."

"Bite your tongue, Hailon."

"It's true!" she insisted with a chuckle. "Besides, I've seen many of your previous suitors and can guarantee that the options are better here than they ever were back home."

"Thank all the saints for that." The number of eligible men in my age range back in Ravenglen was disappointing to say the least. Not that I was even looking, but my mother had seemed positively urgent about matching me once I'd passed twenty-five, and there hadn't yet been a wedding. I was now over thirty, and I'd had to mention that Revalia would have more options for a husband as well as jobs when I'd left, just so she wouldn't be quite so worried.

As if finding a husband would solve anything. It never had for her, though she'd certainly tried. Four separate times she'd tried to claim her eternal happiness, and each time I'd ended up the responsible adult in the house taking care of my much younger siblings, myself, *and* her when her marriage dissolved or blew up.

A stab of guilt hit me in the chest, the same one I'd gotten watching the girls practice with their wooden swords. I'd left my siblings behind. I knew it was for the best, and they'd never begrudge me for it. But I'd been the only stable thing in their lives many times, and now I wasn't there if they needed me again. I'd been selfish for once. The guilt over it was terrible.

By the time we caught up, Seir had already put my bags in the bedroom. The door and windows were all open, and a brisk breeze blew through. The smell of freshly cut lumber was still potent but not unpleasant.

Emotion narrowed my throat. Very few things were ever brand-new in my life, let alone a whole house. And having it all to myself was a luxury I didn't know how to process.

"It's beautiful." I stood just inside the door, almost afraid to move, like the house might vanish if I did, exposing this all as just a lovely dream.

"Come on." Hailon tugged me by the hand and gave me a tour. It didn't take long, the cabin was hardly large, but I grinned like mad as I tried to take in all the little details.

"I think green is the right choice," I muttered, picturing curtains for the kitchen in a soft sage, perhaps a blanket for the sofa in dark pine.

Hailon's mouth twitched. "I brought over some of the basics we had extras of to get you started." She opened cabinets and drawers. "But you can move them wherever you want of course. And if you want new things, I'm sure that can be arranged too."

"These will do fine."

She drew me in for a quick hug and took the canvas back, tacking it to the kitchen wall. "Settle in. Come find me if you need something, okay? You can find your way?"

I nodded. "Yes, I can. Thank you, Hailon." I stared into her eyes so she could feel how deeply I meant the simple words.

"It's my honor, Merry. And I mean that. You were the only person back home to be an actual friend to me. I want you to find your happiness too."

She left after double-checking that I had ample food, that the plumbing was operational so I could get a glass of water and take a bath, and that there was at least one extra blanket for me to use.

As the eldest daughter of a flighty mother, I wasn't used to such attention. Managing all the small details was something I usually took care of. It would definitely take some getting used to, but it was nice to be fussed over.

For at least half an hour I wandered from room to room, touching the fixtures, straightening a pillow here, arranging a towel there, picturing what could be if I had endless funds to spend at the market and this place was truly mine. I tested out one of the new knives on a lovely pear someone had put in one of those pretty little baskets Hailon had been looking at in the city.

As I ate, I walked around the exterior of the cabin, noting that during construction the soil had been disturbed in several places that would make wonderful little garden beds. Planting could still be done for some winter crops if I hurried. A persimmon tree would suit nicely for shade along the back of the cabin, and squash would do well along the far side. I made a mental list for my next trip to the market.

It was fairly early, so I left the little cabin and walked into the glade proper. I stopped to test the five hot springs pools with my hand, then wandered into the area heavy with trees I'd been told had plentiful wild berries. Beyond the edge of that little grove was Hailon and Seir's cabin, but I didn't venture that far. I marveled as I glanced around, the scent of pine heavy on the air and the singing of insects and chatter of birds constant. The area was a true oasis, abundant in every way, and I considered myself blessed to have been invited.

Carrying an overflowing handful of sweet black fruit, I made my way back, unsure exactly what to do with myself. I wasn't used to having such profound peace and free time. I'd never spent a night truly alone before, and never in a place so quiet.

After another wander around the cabin, I put the berries into a small bowl with a handful of seeds and nuts Hailon had left in the cabinet, and took them and a pot of tea with me into the bathroom. I was going to indulge in a long, hot bath. With snacks. It was the height of decadence. The only thing missing was a glass of wine, and I could easily remedy that during my next visit into the city.

As the water filled the tub, wonderfully hot straight from the tap, I gathered my supplies. A pitcher for my hair, the shampoo and soap, an unbelievably plush towel. Unable to stand the wait, I stripped down and climbed in before it was even halfway filled.

Back home, we had a bath of course, but nothing like this. This basin was so large and deep, my knees wouldn't even be above the water if I sank down enough to put my head under. The water was always either scalding or barely warm depending on how impatient I was with boiling pots on the stove that day, and I never had any soaps or shampoos of such high quality. I looked at the door, which I'd closed out of habit. At any given time, someone at home would have been knocking to make me hurry or rushed in to use the toilet. That wouldn't happen here. I could have left it open.

Guilt pressed in, uninvited and unwelcome, demanding to know how I dared to revel in such luxury knowing full well what little my mother and siblings had back in Ravenglen. I frowned, grappling with the emotion. They were housed, fed, clothed. There would be more to go around now that I wasn't there, in fact. Life wasn't always easy, but there was joy. Mother worked, and Mattias would be of age to start at the market soon, or maybe the stables, so that would help. I planned to send some money every month once I found work. I'd left behind what I could, as well. It wasn't like I'd just up and abandoned them with nothing. They could always come to Revalia too.

Before it could take hold again, I shook off the guilt and wave of homesickness that threatened. The heavy feeling in my chest eased, and I sank into the water on a sigh. The bath was everything my body needed after the incident with the owl and the disorienting trip through the portal. I soaked until the water started to cool, then washed in earnest. By the time I moved to get out, I was as relaxed as could be and blinking heavy.

At least, until I reached for my towel and a small, furry creature launched itself at me.

CHAPTER 6
COLTOR

I FOUND MYSELF STANDING in front of the little cabin instead of my own hut.

I'd been lost in my thoughts as I followed the path from the portal through the glade, but I hadn't been *that* distracted.

All the young stone kin working on the other new dwellings had already left for the day, half a hut and a partial cabin completed for their day's labor. I was glad to see they'd heeded my warnings to stick to the paths, sparing the grass and other foliage, but the evidence of their presence still left me feeling oddly intruded upon. The ruins had been mine and only mine so long, having that many people in and out was beyond comprehension. Frowning, I decided to do a thorough inspection of the area during my nightly patrol.

I stared at the cabin, feet planted as though stuck in the mud. I had no reason to be here, yet here I stood.

It was still bright enough out none of the lamps were lit in the windows, and it was too warm yet to need a fire, so there was no smoke coming from the chimney. Signs of life were few, and she very well could have gone with Seir and Hailon to their place, but I got the distinct feeling Merry was inside. After several long moments of internal debate, I decided not to knock on the door—I had nothing to say to her, after all. I did, however, do a quick sweep around the property to be sure everything was in order. It would not do at all for a new guest's security to be left up in the air.

The windows were all open, which made me curious what life had been like in Ravenglen. I wrestled with a flash of anger, reminding myself that there was nowhere safer than here to do such a thing, after all. This was not a city where someone with ill-intent would accept such a thing as an invitation. And as far as I could tell, nothing seemed out of place or suspicious. Besides that, I could trust my kin. I shook my head, frustrated with my tangled thoughts as I headed back toward the path that would lead to my hut.

But I stopped cold at the sound of her scream.

The sound cut jaggedly through me, and before I had time to breathe through the rush of emotions it evoked, it came again but louder, full of terror. Pulse pounding, I spun, limbs pumping. It seemed I'd barely taken a step at all and was already rushing up the few porch steps and through the front door. The main rooms were dark, which was momentarily disorienting. The shrieking noise came again, then a bang, both from behind the closed bathroom door.

My throat was locked up tight with a cocktail of fear and the instinct to destroy whatever had Merry making that sound. Blade drawn and blood up, ready for battle, I threw open the door.

After stepping through the frame, I froze, utterly unprepared for what I found inside the room.

Merry was barely on the outside of the draining tub, dripping wet and clutching a towel to the front of her body. One slight movement, and every last one of her curves would be on full dis-play. I struggled desperately to tear my focus from her glistening skin as I evaluated the situation.

There was a mix of water and tea splashed on the floor, a teacup broken near her feet and an upended pot slowly leaking its contents out into a puddle. Merry defensively held out one of her arms toward a very angry, very wet squirrel perched on its hind legs on the rim of the tub. It chattered and squeaked, cheeks full and tiny chest heaving. They'd both startled at my sudden entrance, but neither moved.

Her eyes darted to me and she tried to adjust the towel to cover more of her body without lowering her arm. "Saints and devils, what are *you* doing here? Do you just walk in anywhere you please?"

"Of course not! You screamed. I came to help. Your door wasn't locked."

She huffed. "Well, as you can see, I'm fine. This little thief scared me is all. He decided to invite himself into my bathroom without permission." She raked her eyes over me. "Seems the pair of you have that in common." The squirrel's gaze darted between us, finally settling on Merry. "He was helping himself to my snack. Startled me when I reached for my towel. We're still having some difficulties figuring out who's going to leave and how. When I move, he moves, and usually in a way that seems like he might jump on me. Again." She scowled at the little rodent, eyes drifting to some scratches on her arm.

"Stay still. There's a broken cup—" I shifted my weight forward and the little creature scampered across the rim of the bath. Clearly panicked, it seemed to be weighing which of us might be the bigger threat. After giving a squeak, he leapt for the window, claws rasping against the wood as he scrambled onto the sill and out the open pane.

Relief flooded her features. "Thank the saints, he's gone. If you don't mind?" Her glare at me was vicious, the towel now wrapped snugly around her frame, one hand holding it together above her breasts. "Coltor, you should leave. Turn around at least."

"Your feet are bare, you can't—"

"I'm fine, I'll just go around—" the length of her thigh was exposed as she attempted to take a step, but found more porcelain shards where she tried to plant her foot.

I rubbed my fist against my thigh, teeth gritted firmly together. Frustration boiled within me, my chest hot and achy, everything in my soul screaming that I need to fly, to fight ... to fuck. For obvious reasons, none of that was possible at the moment.

On fire from the inside out, I stepped forward, avoiding as much of the mess and glass as possible and grabbed her up against me.

"Coltor! Put me down!"

"It's dangerous."

Her complaints were many and loud, but I stopped listening, focused only on getting her away from the danger. I carried her to her bedroom, sat her on the mattress and left the room, closing the door behind myself. While she muttered and opened and closed cabinets, I practiced taking a few full, deep breaths and went in search of a broom to clean up the mess in the bathroom.

She emerged dressed in a fresh tunic and leggings just as I was depositing the last of the glass into the little trash bucket in the kitchen. Her hair dripped wet ribbons down the linen.

"You didn't have to do that." Her tone was still sharp, but lacked bite. She sagged. "But thank you."

"Are you injured?"

"No. Embarrassed, maybe." Her head tilted. "How did you even hear me?"

Her screams echoed in my ears, and the volatile mix of fear and frustration that had finally settled perked up again. "Your windows are open."

Her mouth tilted upward. "They were that way when I got here. Besides, is there a danger out here in the middle of nowhere I should be wary of? Someone who might come into my cabin without warning? Besides you, I mean."

"Besides *me*?" I choked on the word.

"You're the one who decided to just come in here." She frowned, the lighthearted tone she'd taken turning hot again.

"You *screamed*."

"I had it handled." Her bluster infuriated me, but I could see the thread of unease underneath it.

"You should close your windows and lock your doors, Merry."

"I'll take it under consideration, Coltor."

Then, unable to stop going too far, I said, "I was promised I'd hardly know you were here. This is the opposite of that." I regretted the words even as I said them.

Her gaze shuttered, her tone going cold. "I'm sorry about that, but in fairness I had no idea you'd be lingering nearby while I was being surprised by a squirrel. I do truly appreciate you helping, but I think it would be best if you left now. Please."

I obeyed, resigned to ignore the fire raging in my veins that Merry had incited, the irritation at myself for lashing out, for making her feel bad.

As I stomped down the path toward my hut, I scrubbed at my chest, the aggressively powerful beat of my heart strangling my throat through a few breaths. I lingered a moment, making sure there was nobody in the glade but us before I finally moved along, cursing myself the whole way. She had no business invading so many of my thoughts, and going into that cabin now that she was in it was none of mine either. We could keep our separate schedules, go about our own business, and never see one another if we planned it right.

But what was I to do if she was in danger again? Or about my vision of her dying?

Not meaning to, I slammed the door behind myself, making the windows and even the plates in the cabinet rattle. Hands in my hair, I paced the small single room until my thoughts were coherent again. I picked up my most recent wood carving, a duck, but set it back down after I trimmed one of the wings a little too far and nicked my thumb.

There were several hours before true dark, when I needed to be out in the ruins on patrol. There was only one way I was sure to get some rest instead of obsessing over my new neighbor, my visions, and what I was going to do about them.

I sat on the end of my bed, clasped my hands together and forced myself into stone sleep.

I WOKE REFRESHED, but no less burdened by my thoughts. I took to flight immediately once I was outside my little hut, relishing the slight chill on the early autumn air.

Nights in the ruins were my favorite time. Imagined or otherwise, the magic in the old stones seemed to be strongest under the moonlight while most of the creatures in the forest slept.

Castle Emankor had once been a sprawling stronghold, backed by mountains to one side, courted by a river along the edge, and facing the most fertile valley in all of Cyntere. It had been built in the shape of an X, more or less. I would have loved to have seen it when it was whole, such a place was surely nothing short of a spectacle at its height.

Legend was, the old king was a friend of the fae if not fae himself. He'd overseen construction over a lifetime suspiciously long to be simply human, and his magic had been woven into the very stones and lumber he'd built with. Legends were trickly like that, however. It was possible things had been exaggerated or embellished, and those who knew the truth were either fully committed to the lie or long gone.

The old king had held many superstitions if the stories were to be believed, and he'd chosen the shape and many of the decorative patterns specifically to trap any demons that might come through. Wise, if you asked me, but not foolproof. I smirked, thinking of Seir and his brother Tap. Seir was a traveling demon and could go pretty much wherever he cared to at little more than a thought, particularly in Hell, and had a fantastic grasp of portal travel. Tap was in charge of the crossroads, the keeper of all doorways. If the king had known there would one day be a demon living right outside the walls of his castle and another had been in charge of the gates the whole time, he would have been aghast.

Though the old king's reign had long since passed, and the castle had been reduced to not much more than rubble and lore, the magic remained. At the heart of the old building was a central hall, and if one knew where to look between the fallen stones, broken pillars, and encroaching foliage, they could find the doors I'd been assigned to guard.

Much like the portal to Revalia, the doorways could take the user through to another part of the kingdom or another realm entirely. Unfortunately, doorways work both ways—they sometimes also allow things through to our world that we might not want here. Such an event was rare but had happened, so a permanent post had been assigned for a stone kin sentry. Keeping things out that didn't belong, like travelers and creatures from other places, was the whole of my job. It was important. Purposeful. Peaceful.

And much of the time, it was dreadfully boring.

In fact, I'd taken to carving figures out of wood and arranging stones in ever more tediously balanced stacks and arches to keep myself entertained.

The magic itself, however, was always pleasant to be around. It was a light, sparkling presence, proof that the old king's intentions were good, even if he hadn't planned properly for what might happen after he'd departed this plane.

I roamed the perimeter of my wards, ensuring that they were as tidy and strong as they could be. For the dozenth time, I resolved to ask Ophelia if she would deign to leave her hut to help me strengthen them. Hers in the Dread Forest were a true marvel, and with a boost from her power I would feel much better about the ones here. She hadn't left her home even a single time that anyone could recall since moving there, and I'd failed to work up the courage to ask her any of the times I'd visited. Perhaps the next time I'd be brave enough.

After that, I surveyed the road that ran through the boundary. It was not well-traveled, but still hosted unsuspecting wanderers now and then. It had delivered Seir and Hailon into the ruins not all that long ago, as they traveled through on their way north. Next came the castle itself, my wings getting a workout as I lifted myself further above the grounds to get an aerial look at things.

I went through the familiar motions I performed every night: checking, assessing, noting changes or growth. I inspected the new dwellings as planned, and made sure that there was nothing out of place except where it couldn't be prevented. All doorway activity was verified and logged in a tome I kept in a locked box in my hut. I selected some pieces of lumber for carvings and pulled together a group of fairly flat rocks to start a new perfectly balanced pile. The familiar routine was a comfort to me. Not to mention a good distraction from what had happened with Merry.

When the first light of dawn finally crested the horizon, I headed back to my dwelling, eager for a meal and some rest. But not before a detour past the new little cabin, which I discovered still had all its windows open.

AN ITCH PERSISTED under my skin even after I showered and ate. Curious, I went to see if the construction crews had perhaps started arriving early and that's what had my senses alight. Stacks of lumber sat awaiting their craftsmen as they'd been the night before, and the glade as a whole was quiet save the birds and other small animals waking up for the day. I was doubting my instincts until I rounded the last curve of the path and saw her.

Merry was up with the sun, using a trenching spade she found saints knew where. The sharp edge glinted in the sunlight, and I fought against the wave of protective instinct that rose up at the sight. She'd rigged up wooden stakes and string for an outline, and was busily hacking away at the soil to make what looked to be planting beds in large, rough rectangles.

There were also a few birds of prey circling above her. They reminded me of the ones that hung around with the demons at d'Arcan. I wondered if they believed her to be some kind of special snack, her hair a bright beacon under the early morning sun.

I didn't interrupt, though I did stand there longer than I should have, watching her work, making sure the birds didn't make any aggressive moves, and ensuring the blade was always as far as possible from her body as she swung it into the earth. Merry was small but enthusiastic and clearly had plenty of experience working the earth, but still, I wanted to step in, to take the tool from her.

To keep her safe.

I rubbed at the sudden burn under my breastbone with the heel of my hand, unsure how my simple breakfast had left me with such terrible indigestion.

Once she finally set the dangerous tool down, I gave a sidelong glance at the birds, who had stopped circling and were instead perched on her roof. When I looked back, I found myself paralyzed.

In the short moments I'd had my eyes on the new avian visitors, Merry had tugged her blouse off. She wore a thin camisole underneath, but it left very little to the imagination where her form was concerned. For the second time in less than a full day, I tried to remember how to breathe at the sight of her bare flesh. She used the inside of the discarded shirt to blot at her face and neck, then tied it around her waist before doing a final pass around the garden bed. I marveled at her strong shoulders as she put her back to me, hands on her hips. There was a reddish mark near her spine that I leaned forward to inspect closer, catching myself a breath before actually taking a step. When she turned and bent down to inspect something in the dirt, every part of me flushed hot as her ample cleavage tested the fortitude of the rounded neckline and thin straps.

Pulse pounding and a painful ache in my trousers, I cursed my own nosiness. It brought me nothing but grief. Once I could move again, I left her to her business and swore to practice minding mine.

CHAPTER 7
MERRY

ESPITE THE DIFFICULT time I'd had winding back down after the strange interaction with Coltor and the squirrel, I was awake the moment the first rays of daylight spilled through my window. I pulled myself from the impossibly comfortable mattress feeling so well rested it was like I'd slept a week instead of a night.

A slow morning was not really something I knew how to have, so after dressing and a quick tea, I went out to take a walk. Back home, there was always work to do, somewhere to be. Adjusting to no clock ticking in my head, guiding every move I made, was difficult no matter how welcome.

First, I wandered the path between my cabin and the portals. Then, I took another pass by the hot springs, dipping a hand in each of them, amused by the temperature differences despite the way they sat directly next to one another. I wandered further down, taking a peek at the buildings still under construction, curious when the stone kin builders would arrive.

If I hurried, they'd never notice I'd borrowed a few of the tools they'd left lying around.

I collected the items I wanted, then quick-stepped back to the little cabin, hopeful that when it came to something like putting in garden beds, asking permission was unnecessary. If for some reason it wasn't, I'd just do my best to ask forgiveness.

The builders had tossed the string and stake off to the side once they were no longer needed, so I'd snatched them up for my own uses and set about marking off three separate rectangular beds. After that was done, I used the clever trenching spade attached to a rod like a gardening hoe, turning the soil over and defining the shapes of the beds as I worked.

The feeling I was being watched made the skin on my neck tingle. I turned my eyes to the sky, spying some birds circling above me. I glanced around, finding nothing more unusual than a squirrel in a tree nearby—probably my brazen snack thief—and continued working.

It warmed up rapidly as the sun took to the sky, and I was covered in a sheen of sweat before long. I was determined to finish and return the tools, however, so I kept on at as fast a pace as I dared, pleased to find the little beds in decent order after perhaps an hour or so.

I slipped inside to get some water and to wipe a cool wet cloth over my face and neck, then collected everything I'd borrowed and returned it to the construction site. Not a moment too soon either. As I was headed down the little path toward Hailon's cabin, voices chased on the breeze behind me, signaling the work crew's arrival.

There were perhaps two dozen stone kin men and women walking in ones and twos down the path from the portal, smiling and clearly ready to work.

I didn't even need to knock, as it turned out, Seir came around the corner of the cabin with his arms full of firewood just as I approached.

"Good morning!" he greeted me enthusiastically. "Did you rest well?"

I sighed, turning my face into the sun. "Perhaps the best I've ever slept."

His ever-present smile broadened, giving him a dimple as he gestured for me to follow him into their little house. "I think this place is partially responsible."

"And here I thought it was the incredibly soft mattress and the ability to take up as much of it as I wanted, with no sibling stealing my blanket or kicking me in the shins all night."

He laughed outright as he stacked the logs by the hearth. Hailon turned from where she stood in their kitchen. "Merry! Oh good, you're right in time for breakfast."

Not wanting to impose, I waved my hands. "That's okay, I had a little something earlier." Unfortunately for me, the fruit and bread I'd eaten with my morning tea hadn't stuck with me nearly as well as I'd thought, and my stomach whined.

Hailon raised an eyebrow and pointed at their dining table. "Well, that's settled. There's plenty." She leveled me with a look that told me she understood my refusal, but it was unnecessary.

"Thank you."

I sat, the pair of them working together to bring the plates and cups to the table for all three of us. It was marvelous synergy to watch, like they were tethered by an invisible string.

"So, what's on the schedule today?" Hailon asked, buttering a slice of thick toast, then smearing on jam. I absently wondered aloud if I could collect enough of the little black berries to make a batch for myself.

"I bought this jar in the city, but I'm sure there are plenty of berries. I could help you gather some up, along with doing the canning," Hailon offered.

"That would be nice. I ate a few last night, and they're definitely ready."

"What else do you need for that?" Seir asked, clearly thrilled by the prospect.

"Sugar and jars. Perhaps a lemon or two." I shrugged. "Jam isn't complicated."

"Make a list." Hailon nodded. "You always were really good at this kind of thing. Perhaps you can teach me."

"You did just fine, as I recall."

"Not really, we traded for most of our pantry stores. We always focused on ointments and tinctures. Food was very low on the priority list." She waved her fork around thoughtfully as she chewed her toast. "Actually, I'm betting Grace has a whole schedule for buying things like jars and preserving vegetables. We should ask her."

"Perhaps a quick trip into Revalia then? I was also hoping to get some seeds," I said. "The climate here is really very nice, I think if I get some in the ground we could have a decent harvest before a hard frost hits. Rylan seemed to like my suggestions for the gardens at d'Arcan, so I was hoping he could include a request for me when he orders." I had a tiny bit of coin left, hopefully that would be enough.

Seir nodded. "I'm sure that won't be a problem. Coltor said the winters are a bit milder here than Revalia, not to mention somewhere further north like Ravenglen, but the ground still freezes for several weeks at least."

We finished breakfast while making a list of things we'd like to try to grow. Flowers, vegetables, herbs. Nothing was off-limits as long as we could find plants or seeds.

"I've always been good at the collecting part, but the rest was never my strong suit." Hailon sighed, and her vision lost focus as she recalled her life before.

"I'll show you what I know. We'll have your pantry full in no time." I offered her a smile, and she returned it, hope sparking behind her multicolored irises.

"I've got to get going," Seir said, leaning down to kiss Hailon on the cheek as he moved to take his plate to the sink. "I'm meeting with Tap."

"We can walk you," Hailon said. "Leave those"—she gestured to my dishes—"I'll do them when we get back from the city." She grabbed up a satchel, and we all made for the door.

The sound of hammers and saws was audible even from a distance as the stone kin worked on the new cabins.

"They're so *fast*," Hailon marveled. "A couple of days or so per building. It's truly incredible, one day there's basically nothing there, the next there's a whole house."

"They've been slowing down a bit. It's about a day to get the basic structure up, another for walls and such. Another few for plumbing and cabinets. Several more for beautifying touches. I think several of them realized that they enjoy this assignment and if they finish too efficiently, it's going to end before they're ready to move on." Seir's smile was broad. "Can't say as I blame them."

"Who else is being placed out here?" I asked.

Hailon shrugged. "I don't think there've been any official assignments yet."

The screech of a large bird had me looking skyward. It looked like the ones keeping an eye on me earlier were still following me around. I'd counted three, but the small group doing graceful turns on the wind had grown to four. Before, I never would have noticed beyond quiet admiration for how beautiful they were. Now, I was unsure if I should brace for an experience like I'd had with the little owl at Ophelia's, or expect the normal kind of interaction I'd had with the squirrel.

"Hello sir," Seir said jovially to a fat brown rabbit with a fluffy white tail that scampered across the path in front of him.

Then the creature stopped, sat up on his little hind legs, little nose wiggling, and looked me right in the eye. I froze, then I swore. Like the owl it was, then. The hold the rabbit had on me was not as powerful as the little yellow-eyed owl's, but I was still stuck in place.

Friend? The little voice was clear enough.

"Yes, hello. I can hear you." The rabbit accepted my response with a long blink before hopping away.

"Alright, Merry?" Hailon asked.

"Yes, I'm fine." I shook out my shoulders, trying to loosen away the residual sensation of being paralyzed.

Seir stared, but as usual, seemed more amused than surprised. "Hailon didn't tell you?"

"Oh, she did, but it's quite another thing to see it in person." We resumed walking, but at a much slower pace. "You greeted him too. Was that just you being friendly?"

"No, I can hear them too. Though I suspect my ability has more to do with my demon nature than anything else. I've never had a bonded creature. Neither has Vassago, but with a bit of effort, he can hear Rylan's bird as well as Greta's. I'm not sure about Calla's cat, but she's a bit different as she's stone kin."

"Wait, the cat is stone kin?" I recalled the oversize feline that had rubbed against my legs outside the paddock, realizing it had been far more than a cat and I had actually heard it say hello to me after all.

"Indeed, it's fascinating to watch her fly." We approached the portal, and Seir dipped down to kiss Hailon. "My brother Tap manages the contracts for familiars. I'll speak with him."

"Ophelia said she'd be sending him a message as well." I suddenly remembered the leather volume in my bag. "She gave me a book, but I haven't had a chance to read through it."

"Would you be amenable to speaking with my brother directly? You would likely have to travel to him, as he rarely leaves his post, but I could go with you."

"Me too, if need be," Hailon volunteered.

"Yes, of course."

He nodded, pleased by that answer. "Alright. Have fun in town, ladies." Seir kissed Hailon once more and then all but dove into the portal. My stomach heaved.

"Our turn. Shall we?" Hailon held out her arm to me, and I linked it with mine.

"I'd like some seeds, so I suppose we should get on with it." I shuddered.

Hailon laughed and we stepped through together.

OUR TRIP WAS very productive though short. We'd only needed to speak with Grace, who seemed thrilled to share the burden of seasonal food preservation with us.

"I have my little helpers, but the youngest are bored quickly, and it would be lovely to make a day of it. I'll see if the ladies here at d'Arcan would like to join as well. Ah! How exciting. I've not had a proper seasonal preserving party in ages. My mother and aunts used to do one every year until it got too taxing for them."

Grace did indeed have a whole schedule, and she added our needs to the list for d'Arcan while feeding us a whole meal's worth of finger foods with our tea. I could already tell that living here was going to spoil me in no time.

"Let the headmaster pay," she'd said with a wink, calculating far more than I would have both in seeds and canning supplies. I'd learned already how Grace operated and knew it was pointless to argue. Instead, I asked to look at her brilliant chart and we talked about developing a calendar so that we knew what was coming next. Between the expansion that Rylan had decided on for the campus and our little beds, there would probably be plenty to go around all year long.

"Who's going to manage the gardening project?" Hailon asked.

"Bridget said she'd take it on." Grace grinned. "Took some convincing, though. That girl is terrified her thumbs might be black and she'll disappoint Rylan."

"I can help," I found myself offering. "I'm the one who made the suggestions, after all. Once the seedlings are in and growing well, it won't take much effort on her part. Just weeding and watering. Watching for bugs." I shrugged.

"That would be wonderful, Merry, thank you." Grace smiled at me in a way that had me feeling emotional. It was an expression full of pride, one that I hadn't realized I'd been longing for.

After we'd finished up with Grace, Hailon went to discuss something with Greta, and I spent a bit of time with Jacks. I made sure his stall was clean and his needs well met, then I walked him around the paddock and fed him treats. He was arguably going to be as spoiled as I was, living at the collegium. The stableman, Clem, was clearly dedicated to his work and cared for the animals as if they were family. He seemed all too pleased to have another beast to manage, and Jacks had clearly already taken to him. Jacks's approval was good enough for me.

The trip back through the portal felt slightly less distressing, which was hopeful. Hailon's breakfast and Grace's snacks still flipped around in my stomach, but I only had to pause for a moment to settle.

As we approached my cabin, Hailon stopped mid-stride and laughed. "When did you have time to do all this?"

"This morning, before I came to your place."

She strode over to the rectangle of turned soil along the front of the house, kicking at one of the lumps of dirt with her toe. "I didn't realize you'd picked up a hoe or spade."

"I didn't. Not exactly." I laughed at her incredulous expression.

"How did you manage this then?"

"I ... borrowed some things."

"Borrowed? From where?" I gestured vaguely in the direction of the new buildings. Hailon smiled wide. "I'm impressed. But I'm going to tell you what I've learned. It's profound, are you ready?"

"I suppose."

"This isn't Ravenglen."

I choked a laugh. "Obviously?"

"What I mean is, you don't have to sneak anything around here. Just ask for what you need."

I blinked at my friend, the words simple but hard to process. My mind supplied a dozen what-if scenarios at such a bold suggestion. "But—"

"No buts. You saw what happened with Grace, right? She added your things to her list. No questions, no justification, no discussion of payment. Just ask. Me, Seir, one of the stone kin builders. Anyone at d'Arcan. Ophelia, even Coltor. Anybody you've met since you arrived here. Ask. No guilt or explanation required."

"I don't have any *money*, Hailon." The words were hushed, the familiar shame of them making my cheeks burn. I'd said those words to her several times in my life, each time hoping she'd be willing to provide healing or medicine for an offering of bruised produce or a few meals. This somehow felt worse. Right now, I had nothing at all of value to trade, and she'd basically given me a whole new life already.

"Neither did I, remember? What I said still stands. We'll find a way for you to make some coin if you want." She reached out and took my hands. "I promise, Merry. Just ask. This place, these people ... nothing is like it was back home."

Her sincerity soothed my ragged nerves. "I'll do my best."

"Good. Now. Show me what you have planned. Then we can go borrow that trencher again, and you can come over to mine and help me get started too."

I nodded, properly rendered speechless by my friend and grateful all over again.

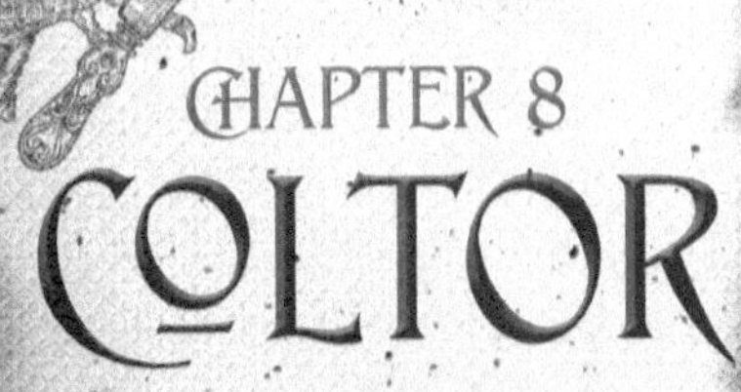

CHAPTER 8
COLTOR

OWN TIME, IT would seem, was not something I would be enjoying.

Between the sounds of hammering and the unusually loud animal noises from outside, I couldn't relax. I resigned myself to the fact that my daylight hours, usually spent sleeping or resting in some capacity, were instead going to be active.

The stone sleep had revitalized me, but I thrived on routine and now mine was being thrown off. It certainly wasn't the worst thing to happen, but I had to work to settle my mood somewhere between disgruntled and neutral before leaving my hut.

I dressed and followed the construction noise to the nearly completed cabins that were close to one another past the hot springs.

"These are looking good," I complimented the crew. They all seemed so young to me, though I recognized a handful of them from several classes below mine at the training academy.

"Thank you," the lead smiled back. He extended his hand to shake mine. "Coltor, yes?"

"That's right. Pleasure to see you again, Neill."

His smile went wide as did his eyes, clearly surprised that I remembered his name. I'd spent very little time at the conclave since my first assignment out of training, but I was good with faces.

As I let go of his hand, I got a little jolt from my gift.

I turned, surveying the construction in progress, trying to picture how and why what I'd seen might happen. Nothing seemed out of place, and stone kin in general were quite hardy. Being equipped with wings and skin that could be turned to stone made us uniquely durable around things like nails and large planks of wood.

Shaking off the vision, I let Neill lead me around the two new buildings. It was clear they all took pride in what they were doing and enjoyed working with one another as well. I noted several names and their particular skills. I'd pass along to my father what I'd seen, though he'd likely chosen them all himself for the very reasons I had noticed them.

Neill walked with me over to the area where the final structures would go, stakes and twine marking off the dimensions. As he finished describing the plans to me, I discovered where much of the noise was coming from.

The whole area around Seir and Hailon's cabin was alight with activity. I frowned, trying to stare through the trees for the cause of such commotion. Then it appeared. The pair of women, both smudged with dirt but with bright smiles on their faces rounded the rear corner of the building.

"Well. I'd best get back to it." Neill clapped me on the shoulder and returned to his work, leaving me there alone. The coward.

Hailon waved, and they walked over. The mixed flock of birds hanging around Merry was now five. Instead of circling above the women, two hawks, a raven, an owl, and a falcon had all perched on the roof to watch instead. A pair of rabbits and a racoon had joined in, and were following them as they walked. My teeth ground together, a distaste for the growing following giving me heartburn.

"We'll be set for planting soon," Hailon enthused. "Merry has our garden beds all planned out. Any requests?"

I eyed the tool Merry had in her hands. It was the same trenching spade she'd been using before. It looked even more wickedly sharp now that I was seeing it up close. My hands ached to snatch it from her, to keep her safe from it.

The chattering and flapping from the animals gouged into my brain like talons, even from a distance. The whole nearby forest seemed alive, thrumming with sound. I couldn't think past it all for a moment and snapped out, "Where did you get this? You could hurt yourself." Merry's expression shuttered, joy replaced by confusion, then anger. The words tasted like acid as they left my tongue. This was not how I wanted to speak to her. Not at all. I just wanted her to be careful. "It's ... sharp." The pitiful addition made me cringe.

Merry's normally bright tone was cool when she addressed me. "I didn't realize using a simple gardening tool, same as I've done my entire life, was such a cause for concern." Her hair caught the sunlight, a fiery halo burning around her.

"It is when you decide to work alone." I put my hand out, and she placed the wooden handle into my palm. Relief at the tool being away from her loosened my chest, but only a little.

"I'm not alone. Hailon has been with me most of the day." Merry crossed her arms, head tilting as she leveled a glare at me. "And I borrowed it from them." She gestured toward the construction crew.

Ribs burning, words continued to fall from my mouth. "You were certainly alone this morning when you were digging all around the cabin you've barely moved into." Her mouth opened, then closed again. "Have you no self-preservation at all? First the windows and doors all wide open, even while you slept and now this?"

"Coltor!" Hailon barked.

Merry was pink in the cheeks, and I could feel the heat of her anger as she glared at me, but that was nothing compared to when she opened her mouth to blister me with her words. "Clearly I *wasn't* alone if you were watching me. And how do *you* know I slept with the windows open?"

My accidental admission was obvious, and there would be no covering it up. "I—"

"And *if* I was, what business is it of *yours*?" Her volume had hardly risen but her tone was cutting.

My pride was wounded, well-earned embarrassment leaving me to stumble over my own words. "It's unsafe to be so casual about—"

"I have no interest in being punished for things you found while performing a security check I didn't request to begin with." She spat the words, and my whole body buzzed like it was full of angry bees. "Or perhaps there's another reason you're creeping around my cabin at odd hours? Walking into bathrooms, checking windows, watching me work? Surely there are easier ways to get a free show?" The angry flush blossomed into her neck and chest, and I felt the full heat of her fury. She held her arms out from her body, the shadows and sunlight making it look like she'd spread her wings. Between that and the halo because of her hair, she had become the embodiment of a firebird.

A stunning, angry firebird.

Hailon was alarmed. "Wait, walking into bathrooms?"

Shame flooded me. I was still messing it all up, but I couldn't seem to stop. It was like I was watching myself fail as tragically as possible from outside my body. "Merry, I—"

"I'm not a child, Coltor, nor a woman who requires someone else to do simple tasks for me. I can use a spade, or a knife for that matter, anytime I wish. And not that I need to justify it to you, but I damn sure can take care of myself. I can even do it scared if I have to, that's nothing new to me. If you have something to say to me, just come out and say it. You agreed to me coming here, even after you were offered alternatives. So if you changed your mind, if you want me gone, ask me to leave. I'll go."

"No, that's not—" I reached out a hand, grasping for any part of the last several minutes back that I could grab.

"Then what I do and how I do it is none of your concern." Merry turned on her heel and strode back toward Hailon's cabin.

Hailon stared at me, expression caught between horror and fury. "What is *wrong* with you?" The words were coated in venom, but true worry came through in her gaze.

"Saints, I wish I knew." I pinched the bridge of my nose between a thumb and forefinger, willing the sudden pounding in my skull to stop. At least the buzzing in my chest had gone.

"Well, figure. It. Out." Hailon's voice never raised, but the words punched at me like she'd shouted them. "Merry's dealing with plenty too, if you hadn't noticed. The city—everything here—is new and strange to her. She's dependent on the kindness of others to get her feet under her, which for her—for any of us, I think—is very difficult to accept. I just barely got through telling her it's fine to ask for help and then you come at her with accusations? For what? Now I look like a liar. I don't appreciate being made to look like a liar, Coltor." Hailon's voice was sharp as it dropped low. "Did you go into her bathroom?"

"I did, but not for no reason, I swear." Her eyes widened. "I'm sorry, I don't know what's happening to me." I scrubbed my hand over my chest, worried my last meal might make a second appearance. "I'm truly not trying to be overbearing, or rude, or make you look like a liar." My insides were all in upheaval, my stomach twisting in on itself, my heart beating a strange rhythm. Even my skin felt too tight and itchy. It took everything I had not to run away, to deploy my wings and fly off to suffer my mortification alone.

Hailon inhaled slowly, her tone deadly when she finally spoke again. "Do you remember what happened last time you weren't trying to be rude? With me?"

I clenched. "I do. Seir put a dagger into my thigh. Despite your quick action and healing talent, I still wear the scar." I'd used it as a reminder more than once, in fact.

"Precisely." She stepped right up to me, her finger poking into my sternum. She only stood as tall as my chest, but that made no difference. "I will personally give you a matching one if you don't mind your manners with my friend." She stepped back, producing her obsidian-handled herb knife from somewhere in her skirts and pointed the blade my direction. "And that's not even considering what she'll do on her own. It would be wise not to underestimate or antagonize her."

"I can see that." She tilted her head, eyes blazing. "I understand, Hailon. I do." I held the useless excuses that sprang on my tongue back, the taste of them bitter. I deserved her ire and owed Merry an apology. She'd done nothing wrong. After several long, silent moments, I asked, "Are the animals acting unusual?" I hoped the change in subject would allow me to recover some of my dignity.

"Yes." Hailon huffed out a breath. "They definitely are."

"They're very noisy."

Annoyance returned to my friend's face. "Can you imagine what it must be like to have them follow you around like they've taken to doing with Merry?"

Surely whatever was happening would also explain the squirrel. "I'm not imagining things?"

"No, you're not. She's collecting creatures. Not intentionally, mind. We're ... working it out."

"Working what out, exactly?"

"You'll have to ask her yourself." She raised an eyebrow, knowing that was a challenge at the moment. "Tap may come through later on. Just so you know. Seir is trying to arrange a meeting for the two of them. We're not sure if it will be here or there."

"Alright." I fidgeted. I couldn't decide whether the idea of another demon—no matter how friendly—coming into the ruins bothered me, or if it was the fact that he'd be doing it because he wanted to talk to Merry that rankled.

Hailon crossed her arms, disappointment and sympathy on her face. "Coltor, I don't understand. I thought you didn't mind Merry coming here—"

"I don't. It's not that. It's not her."

"Then why did you say those things?"

I scrubbed my hand over my face, then tried to do the same with the ache that had returned to my ribs. In the end, I was a coward and gave the simplest explanation, but not one that included my messy feelings about Merry. "The noise," I said. "There's so much lately. I just … it's like daggers inside my skull."

"Well, I'm sorry about that, truly, but it's no excuse for your behavior."

"I know. Please tell her—"

"You can apologize to her yourself. And you should, she deserves a *proper* apology. But not now."

"Of course. I am sorry, Hailon."

Her shoulders sagged. "I believe you. I'm sure this is a lot to deal with."

Hailon pulled me into a quick hug, carefully avoiding the sharp tool I still held in my hand. She then turned toward her cabin, throwing me one more warning over her shoulder with her eyes.

Once she'd gone through the door, I dropped my chin to my chest as I took several slow breaths. I hated the way I felt when I had outbursts like that. And I hated the way I made others feel when I lashed out infinitely more.

After a moment, I went back toward where Neill had resumed work on the cabins. I tossed the tool onto the ground near several others. "Can I be of any help?"

Neill smiled and clapped me on the back, and I joined in the group that was moving planks and other supplies from near the portal to the site. The joyful attitude of the crew, and the way they immediately accepted and appreciated my efforts smoothed a bit of the edge to the racket they created while they worked. Walking along the paths, using my muscles in a way I didn't normally and having a simple job to accomplish helped clear my head. Guilt had its claws in me something fierce for what I'd said and done. I could make it right, though. I would.

As we set the last stack of planks down, I turned and could only watch in horror as my earlier vision played out right in front of my eyes.

I shouted, hand raised as I sprinted back toward the cabin, but it was too late. The stack of large roof tiles someone had piled up while our backs were turned cascaded from the peak down the slope, catching one of the men right in the shins. He was agile and propelled himself away from the heavy stone tiles, but it was not enough. Everything happened too quickly for him to truly deploy his wings, and even his shift was barely half-managed before he hit the ground. In what seemed like no more than a few breaths, he'd gone from working peacefully to having fallen off the roof. As I approached, I knew what I would see but wished not to. I sucked in a breath, finding one of the offending tiles broken and punched through his body, right in the soft place below his collarbone near his shoulder. He wheezed, blood seeping both from the wound and from between his lips as he moaned a curse.

"Infirmary at the conclave. Now," I ordered, and the four men standing closest, all of whom had momentarily been frozen in surprise, carefully collected the injured man between them. We all made for the portal as quickly as we could, paths be damned.

The stone kin settlement no longer felt like home to me, but I knew if anyone could help the unfortunate builder, my sister could.

COLTOR

I RANG THE BELL to summon Lovette to the infirmary as the men deposited the injured man on one of the cots. There were empty beds made up with clean linen all down each side of the room, and the smell of antiseptic clung to the air.

"Go on back and finish up. I'll stay," I offered, and they all filed back out seconds before my sister barreled through the door, not even glancing my way as she collected supplies and rinsed her hands in something that smelled like the rot gut alcohol we'd snuck into the barracks during training.

"I rarely get a ring this time of day. Lucky I was in, normally I'd be—" Her mouth dropped open as she finally looked up. "Coltor? What a lovely surprise!" She strode over, arms wide. I couldn't help but return the bright smile she offered when she saw me, but then she noticed the patient. Her arms dropped before she had a chance to hug me, diverting her course to the side of the cot. "Oh, dear. Emry, right? What's happened to you, then?"

The man could only wheeze, so I answered for him. "He fell off a roof."

"I see. Let me just have a peek, okay?"

I'd rarely seen my sister so in her element as she was inside the infirmary. There was no hesitation in any of her movements as she maneuvered Emry onto his side, her hands deftly prodding around the tile that protruded from his flesh on both sides of his body. Pride lit up my chest as I watched her work.

"Coltor?"

"Mmm?"

"Go wash up." She gestured to the basin she'd stopped at near the door. "I need your help pulling this out. It's missed a lot of important bits, but it's gone through his lung."

"I—"

"Go."

There was no room to argue with Lovette's tone. I felt a bit dizzy when I looked back over my shoulder to see that she'd given him a leather strap to bite down on.

"The tincture will help with the pain, but it's going to take a moment to start working," I heard her tell him, and he grunted in understanding.

I did as she asked, scrubbing with the gritty soap at the basin, the potent liquid burning as it found every scratch and cut in my skin. We crowded over poor Emry once my hands were clean, my heart pounding behind my ribs.

"Hold here." She guided my hands and then met my eye. "Ready?"

"No."

"Don't be shy, I've seen you do this same procedure before with my own eyes." She turned her gaze to Emry, everything about her features softening for her patient. "I promise it's fine, Emry. He's just a little nervous."

The man's eyes were wide as they darted between us. "She's not wrong, I have actually done this before." What neither of us said was that the last time it was a tree branch due to a flying accident. And the patient, my dear friend, had not survived.

"See? On three, pull straight back. Understand?"

"Yes." I braced myself, and she counted down.

Grunting, we both pulled as hard as we could on the tile, but it didn't want to move. Emry groaned, panting around the leather in his mouth. Lovette put a hand against his shoulder and he calmed. Her gift of alleviating fear came in very handy in her work.

"I'm so sorry, Emry. I'm afraid we have to act a bit more drastically." Lovette's tone was serious, and Emry nodded. My lunch churned in my gut as she went back to the supply cabinet, returning with what amounted to a fancy hammer and a towel. She turned to me, voice barely above a whisper. "Remember when Imogen dropped that half-done pot metal blade through her foot when she was an apprentice? And then it broke when she tried to pull it free?"

I swallowed, throat thick as the old memory surfaced. We hadn't had a healer like Lovette running an infirmary back then. In fact, that might have been one of the incidents that pushed her into taking the training. "Yes."

Lovette nodded, her golden curls bouncing against her cheeks as she placed the towel over the bit of tile poking out of Emry's front. "This is going to be like that. You pull, on three."

"Alright." I dabbed the cold beads of sweat from my brow with my sleeve before gripping the tile again.

"Put your foot up on the bed," she said, tone uncomfortably smooth, clinical. "If he rolls backward, you need to brace him with your knee."

"Are you sure someone else shouldn't be—"

"You're doing fine, big brother. Don't forget to breathe, though. Wouldn't want you passing out. I won't be able to catch you, and if you crack your head on the floor, we'll be in trouble." She smirked at me. I was going to catch an absolutely devastating hard time about that from her later, I was certain of it.

"One. Two ..." On three, Lovette raised the hammer up and brought it down with all her might, landing a perfect hit on the tip of the tile piece, just as I pulled backward. Emry shouted over the leather as the tile pulled free of his body with a grotesque sucking sound. I was not ready for the abrupt shift in tension, and landed flat on my ass on the hard stone floor, tile in my hands. "Perfect!" Lovette immediately began tackling the new wound, applying drops of shimmery liquid from a tiny vial, then an ointment that smelled like old gloves before wrapping him in clean bandages.

Emry was dripping sweat but still conscious when she finished, and he managed to give her a thumbs-up and a little grin before slipping off to stone sleep so the healing could speed along.

My sister offered me a bloody hand to help pull me back to my feet. "Not bad for your first surgery out of the field. Though you could have simply come visit, you know."

"Trust me, this is definitely not how I planned to see you," I sighed.

She snorted a laugh. "Come on then. Let's get you cleaned up. Imogen will be so sad she missed this."

I cringed. "She'd have been a better assistant. I could have fetched her from the forge."

"Nonsense. You did perfectly, and she's busy with her fire and steel. Here," she said, scrubbing us both down elbows to fingernails with soap and a small brush. Once she was satisfied, I was rewarded with a bright smile and one of her hands against my cheek. "Well. Look at you."

I stuttered, realizing that she had tears in her eyes. "Lovette, listen—"

"Shut up," she chuckled, scrubbing her tears away. "I haven't even missed you that much, you rotten brute. And I'm certainly not mad that you've been avoiding me."

My little sister, who stood perhaps two full heads shorter than me but who'd always had a personality bigger than life itself, punched me hard—right in the same place Emry had been impaled by a rogue roof tile. Then she threw her arms around my middle and squeezed.

"IT'S NOT LIKE we haven't seen each other," I protested as she dragged me through the meetinghouse, collecting everything she insisted we needed for a proper catch-up.

"We've seen each other for perhaps half a minute several times, that's true," she argued, piling sliced meat and cheese onto a plate. "But there's always been a bunch of people around or somewhere urgent to be. I haven't actually gotten to sit down and talk with you in months." Her bright blue eyes fixed on mine as she placed several bottles in my arms. "I'm well aware that's not your favorite thing, but I'm owed. You'll survive an evening in with your sister ... sss. Sisters. Probably. Maybe." She tucked a whole loaf of bread under her chin and stalked out of the meetinghouse, hands full of overloaded plates and me ambling behind with all the drinks.

"Wait, Imo's coming too?"

"Yes, assuming of course she's finished with her project and doesn't already have dinner plans. She comes by quite a lot, unlike any of my brothers. Only the Fates know when I might actually get to see my *twin*, the bratty worm." She shook her head, curls bouncing.

My thoughts spun as I came to terms with how differently my day had gone than I expected.

"Nice to see you Coltor!" Jorna, one of the aunts who ran the kitchen, called after us with a chuckle.

At least we were between mealtimes, and there were only a

couple of people gathering snacks like ourselves. I didn't think I would have fared well if the hall had been full of my kin. I'd visited once, shortly after Seir had proven he could mind my post for me. I'd lasted long enough to bumble my way through greetings to a very loud and enthusiastic group of revelers enjoying some kind of party, greet my father, kiss my sisters on their cheeks, and leave again. It took me a solid week to recover.

"Of course she is. Do you really think nobody dashed over to the forge to gossip the second you walked into the infirmary?"

Her pace was nothing short of speed walking, always had been. I was using my longest strides to keep up with her as we passed the infirmary door, then went around the corner of the building to a staircase that led up to her apartment.

Another thought occurred as we approached the door. "Is Gaius here?" My sister had found her mate not long before, and while I didn't necessarily dislike the man, the two of us in a room together would likely provide some tension as we maneuvered our new familial ties.

"No. He's at the outpost, like always. They can't seem to keep enough staff to save themselves." She huffed a little, frustration obvious. "You're stuck with us girls this evening." Lovette used her toe to nudge the door open, revealing Imogen already sitting comfortably on the plush sofa. "You're here!"

Imogen returned Lovette's smile. I enjoyed seeing that their bond had grown in my absence. "I should have checked the meetinghouse, I could have helped," she said, making room for the plates and cups on the low coffee table.

"No need, we're all set," Lovette said, appraising the spread before heading into the adjoining kitchen. "I'll just get some utensils."

Imogen's head tilted as she took me in with her eyes, then her arms. Her grip was as impressive as ever because of her work as forge mistress. Her forearms might even have gotten bigger than mine. "Nice to see you, little brother."

"You look well, Imo."

"She's practically radiant lately," Lovette snickered from behind her.

"Hush." Lovette only laughed harder at Imogen's protest.

"Have they got a name?" I asked. A lightness came over me, the banter between me and my sisters comfortable.

"Brom," Lovette supplied helpfully, returning with a fist full of silverware.

Horrified, I straightened. "The mason?"

"Saints, no," Lovette laughed and Imo cursed at me. "The other one."

Relieved that my sister hadn't started dating a relic, I sagged, considering who else it could be. "The leathersmith?" My brows drew together. He was at least around our ages and not a hunched old man.

"That's the one."

"Lovette." Imo sighed deeply, clearly having had this particular conversation with our little sister several times.

"It's hilarious every time, though!"

Imogen rolled her eyes. "For you. Why is it that everyone assumes I'd be attracted to Old Brom in the first place? That's insulting. To both of us, honestly."

Lovette laughed, the cheerful sound drawing a smile out of me. "They're adorable together," she assured me. "Make yourself comfortable."

We obeyed our incorrigible little ray of sunshine and spread ourselves out on her furniture, plates and cups of ale doled out in an old, familiar rhythm.

"So? What's new out at the ruins?" Lovette asked.

I groaned. "Too much."

"It's nice though, right? Well, accidents that bring you here with injured, aside. At least you've got some help. You can leave now and again."

I nodded, the flavor of the roasted meat so specific to stone kin cuisine it triggered several layers of nostalgic memory. "Seir's presence is very helpful."

"But?" Imogen asked.

"But they're building new homes. There will be more people there soon. I'm not used to it."

"Everyone on that project that I've encountered speaks very highly of the location."

"You're welcome to visit," I found myself offering. "The glade is very peaceful. Hopefully it stays that way."

"Why wouldn't it? There are only a few other dwellings, right? And none of them inhabited. Seir and Hailon aside." Lovette sipped on her ale.

"Hailon's friend Merry has taken one of the cabins." My heartburn flared from the spicy meat, and I rubbed at my chest. My sisters shared a look. One that meant nothing but trouble.

"The one that was staying with Ophelia for a bit, right? What's she like?" Lovette asked.

I shrugged, unable to stop the memory of her in that towel from appearing in my mind. "Human. Red hair. Likes to garden."

"She must be something special if Ophelia took her in." Imogen reached for a slice of cheese.

"I guess. Though she's prone to unsafe behavior and attracts noisy woodland creatures." I held my breath, my heart doing that strange pounding in my throat again. Both of my sisters stared at me, then one another. "What?"

"Is she pretty?" Lovette asked, batting her eyelashes.

"I suppose." It almost hurt me to speak so casually about her beauty.

"Does she carry a blade?" Imo asked, leaning forward curiously.

"Aside from the dangerous garden tool she was using the other day, not that I know of. Wait, what is this exactly?"

"Nothing, nothing. Just small talk," Lovette assured me. She grinned, her expression positively unsettling. "When can we meet her?"

I shrugged. "Whenever you like. She's at d'Arcan often, keeps her horse there. Or you can always come directly to the glade. Our portal is getting far more use than your infirmary, by the looks of things."

"Maybe I will." There was no telling if Lovette was kidding or not, and I wondered if I would regret my offer.

The conversation moved on to other things for a bit—what I'd seen at the ruins, the feasibility of Ophelia leaving her hut to help me with my ward. Talk veered back to Merry about the time I decided I needed to get on my way.

"There's nothing else really I can tell you about her."

"If you say so," Imogen said, eyebrow raised.

"Why do you keep staring at me like that?" I asked, glancing between my sisters as I rubbed at my chest. The burning would not subside, no matter how much other food I ate or ale I drank.

"Because you're hiding something." Lovette crossed her arms, her gaze dropping momentarily to my chest.

"I'm not." My body protested the lie, a significant part of me eager to share the burden of my visions, my gift.

"You are. But I think it's because you're scared." Imogen relaxed back into the cushions of the sofa, expression serious. "How interesting."

"No." The bees suddenly appeared inside my chest again with the lie. "I'm not," I insisted.

"How are your lessons with Ophelia going?" Lovette asked.

"What do you know about that?" I barked.

She only snorted at my outburst.

"Your visits to the sorceress are not a secret, Coltor. What other reason could take you there so often? So. What is it you've learned that's got you so twisted up?" Imogen asked.

Panic settled in, smothering the anger that had started to rise up. If I couldn't trust my sisters, who could I trust? They were smart, capable. They'd both been students of Ophelia's as well. Maybe they knew something I didn't.

After much internal debate, I chose faith in my sisters. I vented and cursed and complained all over them and myself, as much as I could without exposing my gift in its entirety. Such a thing was too dangerous to be common knowledge, especially as I hadn't yet mastered it. I focused on my fear of Merry—or anyone else, now that Emry had landed in the infirmary—coming to harm, the amount of distracting noise I was struggling with. How I'd barked at Merry not meaning to, invaded her privacy trying to help after hearing her scream. Imogen nodded sagely, and Lovette chirped encouraging words. They didn't minimize my frustration, but they also didn't have an answer for it.

"That sounds really difficult, Coltor. I'm sure you'll figure it out though." Imogen reached across the table and patted me on the shoulder. "We're always here, for whatever you need."

"You should ask Greta about an elixir," Lovette suggested. "If anyone is injured, you have a whole host of healers you can turn to. Me, Hailon, the archmage ... his whole household, basically. But perhaps there's something she can make up as a preventive. Or a charm maybe, from the archmage? Something to put your mind at ease a bit."

"That would require you speaking to Merry about your worry, of course. Being honest. And apologizing for your earlier, perhaps less-rational reactions to your fear. Surely there's a good reason for it?"

Both of my sisters stared at me as though they were waiting for me to have an epiphany. But I was just as perplexed as I had been after talking with Ophelia. Disappointed, they looked at one another, and a short time later, we said our goodbyes.

Imogen was right though. Our conversation had brought me back to my original dilemma, and I was in a right foul mood about it the rest of the night.

How exactly do you go about telling someone you've had a vision of them dying?

CHAPTER 10
MERRY

"Tap is ... overwhelmed. It's getting better, but be warned that sometimes conversations with him can be a bit confused. Scattered. His mind moves from one thing to the next without finishing sometimes, but he always comes back around eventually." Seir smiled softly, and in it I could see the affection he had for his brother. "He's managing a lot, always has. Coltor and I have been able to relieve some of his burden, but perhaps you can offer aid of a different kind." He led me toward the portal, glancing over his shoulder at the animals that had followed us from my cabin. "There are ... a *lot* of them, aren't there? Good morning, everyone!" He waved at them cheerfully.

There were now seven birds, the two rabbits, a racoon, a family of quail, and a young deer following me around the glade. I caught the birds sleeping on my roof and the rest huddled around my porch when I left.

A carving of a hawk had also been sitting on the railing right next to the stairs. I could only assume it was some kind of peace offering from Coltor. I'd left that right where I found it.

"Yes, it seems there's something new following me every time I turn around. I have to keep my eyes either straight ahead or on the dirt so I don't accidentally make eye contact. I can still hear some of them, though, even if we don't look at one another." That had been a surprising development, but also comforting. The voices weren't nearly as troublesome when they didn't come with a side of paralyzation.

Each of them had communicated with me at some point, and all had left me frozen for at least a few moments as they made contact. It was disconcerting still, but I was getting better at preparing myself when I sensed a new creature near me. None of them had done more than greet me, though I'd gotten several variations of requests. Mostly the request was some combination of the words *help* and *friend*. I felt terrible that I had no clue what to do for them.

"May I?" Seir asked, gesturing at my arm. "I just want to be sure we both end up where we should."

"Oh. Sure."

He tucked my arm through his, patting it reassuringly as we stepped right up to the edge of the portal. "Ready?"

"Yes."

"Let's g—"

His word was cut off as he took one big step, pulling me with him into the magical doorway. I gripped his arm and screamed internally as the portal turned me inside out and sideways, then back again all in the span of seconds. Together, we stepped out into a wide hall filled with other doorways.

"Welcome to the crossroads," an unfamiliar low voice intoned.

I blinked and sucked in a slow breath through my nose as I oriented myself, willing my breakfast to stay put. I was going to have to start traveling with snacks in my pockets and forgoing meals if portals were in my plans. Seir embraced the tall man after pulling his arm from mine.

"Merry, this is my brother Tap. Tap, this is Merry."

Tap bowed his head slightly. His black hair was trimmed close to his scalp to above his ears, then longer on top. Some of the longer strands fell into his eyes when he bent forward. "Pleased to meet you, Merry."

"Thank you for inviting me."

Seir smiled encouragingly at me as Tap turned, leading us away from the hallway to a cozy sitting room. He was built much like his brothers, tall and broad through the shoulder, but slimmer than the others. I'd never met so many large men as I had since arriving in Revalia. Between demons and stone kin, there wasn't a single one that didn't tower over me by at least a head and a half, and I didn't consider myself small.

He gestured to the furniture. "Please, have a seat." Seir and I sat at opposite ends of the new-looking long sofa, and Tap took the worn leather chair for himself after serving us all tea.

"Seir tells me you've recently started hearing animals?"

"Yes. The first time it happened I was with Ophelia. She explained a few things and gave me a book." I'd managed to read some of it after getting back to my cabin the night before, but I wasn't sure I really understood what it said. Getting angry with Coltor and venting about the whole maddening interaction, not to mention explaining what had happened when he came into my bathroom over dinner with Hailon and Seir had taken quite a bit more energy out of me than I'd thought. By the time I'd gotten around to reading, the words had all blurred together. "They don't say much, and being paralyzed when they make eye contact is a bit disorienting, but I don't feel threatened at all."

"The sorceress sent me a letter. She said you've only recently developed animal mind speech?" His tone was matter-of-fact, and his gray gaze curious as he pushed his round spectacles back up his nose.

"That's right."

Tap nodded, the small metal rings he wore in his ears tinkling together with the movement. "I thought I was keeping up with familiar contract requests pretty well, but it would seem I've fallen inexcusably behind." He sighed. Tap's manner was careful and controlled, his voice low and breathy. I got the impression it would take quite a lot to rile him. Tap seemed in every way complementary and opposite to the bundle of enthusiastic energy that Seir was.

Seir, uncharacteristically silent to that point, was staring at his brother empathetically. "You've been very overworked."

"Yes, well, be that as it may, I'm afraid there's quite a mess to untangle. Would you be interested in taking a project on, Merry?"

"I'm not sure," I answered honestly. "In truth, I don't know what any of this means."

Tap smiled, exhaustion evident in the fine lines near his kind eyes. "Fair enough. I can tell you that it's not at all glamorous, the hours are terrible, and the clients can sometimes be … unpredictable." He stood, and gestured for us to follow. "Let me show you the files first." He paused. "Seir? Would you mind watching the doorways?"

"If Merry is alright with that." He raised an eyebrow in inquiry.

"I'm sure we'll be fine, thanks."

With a courteous nod, Seir went back toward the broad hallway of doors while Tap took me into a large side room.

My heart thudded, excitement mixing with incredulity as I scanned the floor-to-ceiling shelves that stretched toward a very, very high ceiling. There was a rolling ladder, and I'd always wanted to use one of those, but I'd never been permitted into the section of the library that had one back in Ravenglen.

The reality of the situation hit me quite suddenly as I tried to comprehend the scale of the space. I was with not one but two demons. We were at the crossroads, a place between worlds, discussing a job that involved contracts for magical familiars. Animals, that could talk to me, in my head. No part of that should make sense, never mind be something I was experiencing given the mundanity I'd lived for the majority of my life. And the strangest part is that I was seriously considering it.

"These are the files." Tap gestured around the room, the rings on his fingers glinting in the bright lamplight. "As are these." He pointed to a stack of wax-sealed parchment letters and envelopes mounded on top of what could have been either a massive desk or a table. It was hard to tell, as nearly none of it could be seen. "And these." Another pile, this time on the floor. "And these." Boxes shoved underneath the flat surface. "There are likely more I haven't sorted out yet in the deals library." The more he located, the further his face fell. I could see the disappointment in his handsome features. The lines of his face were much sharper than Seir's, but there was no mistaking that he belonged with the other demons I'd met, no matter how different all of their appearances were.

"Oh my." My chest felt tight from overwhelm looking at them all.

"Indeed."

"This explains why they seem so anxious to speak to someone."

Tap grimaced. "Apologies for that."

"It's alright, just came as a surprise is all. What would I be required to do?"

"Mostly it's matching things up. The old files can be rotated out, that's these here." He indicated the wall of shelves on either side of the fireplace. Some of the paper was so old it was disintegrating, and many of the documents near the top of the shelves were in scroll form. "That will give us space to get the new contracts organized. That's where you'd come in, I think."

"I can manage paperwork, that's no problem." I'd helped the Grummonds in the office at the grocers back in Ravenglen a time or two.

"While you sort, you'd need to give a quick skim to make sure the creature and the mage are compatible. I can give you a list to cross-reference against. Generally speaking, if they're asking, the pairing is already considered a match, but there're a few things we need to look for. Then I'll sign off on it and we can file them away."

"What kind of things would I be looking for?"

Tap waved his hand with a gentle flourish. "A fish familiar would not do well bonding with someone who lives somewhere a body of water can't be found within several days journey, for example."

"I see."

His gaze went distant and a soft, lopsided grin tugged on his mouth. "I once signed off on a bond between a mage who lived on an island far out in a very turbulent sea and a bear." He grimaced. "Poor Gordon had to devise a whole system of boats and ropes to get Bren across the water to his home. And Bren never wanted to stay." Tap chuckled, a dark rumble in his throat. "He wanted his forest, trees, rocks ... everything the little island with its constant storms and howling winds could never—" He paused, looked at me as though embarrassed to have diverted the conversation in such a way and shook his head. "Suffice to say I've learned many lessons the hard way, and I'm happy to spare you the same trouble."

I glanced around again, the gravity of such a job weighing on me. "How much time would I be expected to devote to the work each day?"

Tap shrugged. "As much as you care to. I'm behind, that's certain, but I don't expect anyone to keep the schedule I do. That would be cruel." His barely perceptible smile faded, and he became thoughtful. "I must apologize, Merry. This office was once very comfortable, but until things are better ... Well, I'll admit there's not much besides mess and dust to be found here right now. Once the contracts are all caught up, that will improve and then maintaining it all will be easier."

That was an enticing offer, to be sure. "Pardon me for being crass, but what about pay?"

He rubbed along his jaw with his thumb and forefinger. "I'll have to consult with my brothers to be sure what I have in mind is fair, but it would be well worth your time."

I knew enough about how Rylan managed his staff thanks to Grace to accept his words at face value.

"Are all the animals trying to speak with me someone's familiar?"

He shook his head, earrings chiming again. "Highly unlikely given the amount and variety Seir has told me are hanging around. I'd imagine a few might be, and the rest are just happy to have found someone who can understand them."

"Seir can hear them too though, and the others who have their own creatures. Why do they only"—I hesitated, trying to find the right word—"swarm around me? Why am I so interesting to them?"

Tap shrugged. "That's a mystery I'm afraid I'm not prepared to solve. Hopefully understanding will come in time." He led me out of the office, back to the little sitting room. "You can take whatever time you need to consider; we can make arrangements when you decide."

"I am. Decided, I mean. I'd like to help them as much as I can. And you too, I suppose."

That gentle, tired smile reappeared. "That's wonderful news, Merry. Thank you."

Seir peeked around the doorway at that moment, very clearly having been eavesdropping. "I'll bring you back whenever you want until you get comfortable doing it yourself. And I'll do my best to try and convince the creatures to give you some space. They really do seem mostly curious about you, about being your friend. How exciting!" He pulled each of us under an arm for a hug. "This is going to be great!"

I laughed at his enthusiasm, thanked Tap for meeting with me, and followed Seir back through the halls of doors to the one for the glade.

For the first time, I didn't mind so much the way it felt going through.

CHAPTER 11
MERRY

IT TOOK SEVERAL days before I felt comfortable in the office at the crossroads. Every time one of the ancient documents gave way and crumbled to dust under my fingertips, my heart lodged in my throat. I had no idea how important such things were, especially the ones that old, but it seemed tragic to lose a piece of history just because I'd disturbed it. They'd been here long before I'd existed, after all.

The first couple of times, I'd made enough noise that Seir had peeked in to check on me. Assured I was still on the ladder and in one piece, he flashed me a smile and disappeared again. He was helping his brother manage the doorways while also keeping an eye on me as I scaled the deceptively tall rolling ladder.

The ladder itself had surpassed all expectations. Instead of separate rails, there was one that continued around the entire room. I would absolutely roll around all day if left to my own devices.

The third time I let out a very unladylike squawk, Tap himself appeared in the doorway. "Is everything alright in here, Merry?" Concern laced his soft tone.

My face itched from the dust, and a warm flush bloomed up my neck. "Yes! I'm sorry. I'm fine. I apologize for interrupting you, I know you're busy. It's just, they keep falling apart." I held up a sad parchment tatter, the rest of the document still sitting on the shelf. A sneeze suddenly burst from me, sending a plume of dust into the air.

The corners of Tap's mouth tipped upward, but he didn't offer the reflexive blessing like I would. I found myself smiling, realizing that such a thing might be odd for a demon to do.

"I should have warned you about the documents," he said. "Don't worry yourself, they have a habit of doing that after so long. What you're able to pack up will be sent for long-term storage in the archives but losing some of the oldest is expected. For the most part, anything not issued within the last several decades will never need to be referenced, so the loss is not devastating. Besides, the parties involved in the bond all have a copy as well." He nodded sagely as he clasped his hands behind his back. That specific posture reminded me of Vassago so much I snorted. He tilted his head, eyebrows drawn together. "Have I said something amusing?"

My blush became full blown, and I climbed all the way down off the ladder, brushing my hands on the light apron I'd found to put over my clothes. "No, it's only that you looked very much like your brother just then."

He frowned, confused. "Seir?"

"Vassago."

Tap's mouth opened, then closed again. His expression went through several transformations before he put one hand over his heart and let loose a raspy laugh that was louder than I expected it to be. I was startled at first, but then laughed with him, the new pose furthering the similarity.

"Posh cad. Though I suppose I could do far worse. What was it, exactly?"

"The way you were standing." I imitated both poses, badly, but well enough to show what I meant. "And you hold your arms in a very similar way."

He put his hands on his hips, then self-consciously crossed them. Giving up, he dropped one to his side and used the other hand to bump his glasses up his nose. "Well. In any case, don't worry yourself about the ones that fall apart. Perhaps work your way up instead of down? They'll reorganize them how they like in the archives anyhow. We can assist you later with the more fragile ones. I'll ask Seir to help remove the crates as you fill them."

Things went much smoother after that, and I worked faster, no longer terrified of things crumbling in my hands.

When we returned home that first night from the crossroads, my collection of animals waited politely a short distance from the portal.

"We've discussed this," Seir told them, shaking a finger at the lot as he gently scolded them. "Go on. Give the lady some room." Several of the small creatures backed into the grass or trees, and a few of the birds took flight.

"They'll still turn up outside the cabin." I smiled despite the strain they were putting on me. I couldn't blame them. Not really. If I wanted to be heard and finding a conduit like I apparently was to make that happen was right in front of me, I'd keep it within sight when I could too.

Seir and I walked down the path together, animals quietly creeping along behind us.

"Whatever they need from you, they're not willing to share with me."

"You asked?"

He nodded. "I have. My mind speech is not the most practiced, but I get by. They understand me fine, but they seem very set on speaking with you specifically. It seems very much like ... loyalty? I'm unsure how to explain it."

"I appreciate you trying." Truly, I was flattered that he had. It made me feel less alone in this odd circumstance.

"You did well today. Are you planning to go back tomorrow?"

My head was throbbing and my legs ached. I'd been very busy without realizing quite how much. "Yes. Can you take me after breakfast? I need to get back early enough to see Jacks, I don't like going too long between visits."

Seir grinned and nodded, pausing as we arrived at the split in the path. "Of course. You're welcome to come to our place to eat. Hailon loves having you."

"I'll do that. Thanks." He raised a hand in a wave as he continued straight, and I took the curved path toward my cabin.

When I got to my little porch, I noticed that a quail carving had joined the hawk. My mouth twitched. Still, I left the little tokens of apology from Coltor as they were.

I also suspected that the extra eyes I'd started to feel following me around had less to do with the animals camouflaged by the fauna than they did the sulky stone kin I believed was keeping watch from a distance.

It should have bothered me far more than it did.

WORK DAYS AND weekends weren't the same concept at the crossroads that they were in the city, but I told Seir I'd be taking a couple of days to rest after returning to the library for five straight, full days. The work was satisfying, even if I'd developed a chronic headache, my whole body hurt from the lifting and bending, and I had a sneezing fit at regular intervals.

He had just returned from one of his seemingly endless trips through a door in the wide hall full of portals to deliver a massive crate of contracts to the archives somewhere in Hell when I mentioned my ailments.

Seir paled. "Oh, Merry. I've made a terrible mistake, I'm so sorry."

I laughed, thinking he was about to make a joke. "Oh?" I wiped my perpetually dry, dusty hands on a cloth I kept in the pocket of my apron. "It's not that bad. I'm probably out of shape, maybe a little allergic to parchment dust."

"No, it's not that. Though I'm sorry that you're uncomfortable at all, and Tap will be as well. But I didn't think to mention the time because I'm used to it. It honestly didn't occur to me at all."

"Time?"

Seir sagged, the apologetic look on his face pitiful. "Time passes differently here. We leave in the morning and return in the evening in the glade, but here, about an hour and a half passes for every hour there. You've been working much longer than you thought." He grimaced, horrified.

I considered this. Time hadn't felt like it was passing any differently, but I'd been so busy I wasn't paying much attention. I was seeing progress, and every day it got harder to want to leave in what felt like the middle of my project.

"Oh. Well, that explains some things, but it's alright. Knowing wouldn't have changed anything."

He apologized twice more, then grabbed up another crate.

Sore and exhausted but also immensely proud, I'd continued on that day until I finished the whole wall. The shelves were all empty, wiped free of old dust, and ready for the new files to be installed.

"A job well done." Tap offered his compliments as Seir and I prepared to go home. "Please accept my most sincere apologies. I'm embarrassed to have omitted several things accidentally, and very grateful for your efforts."

"It's fine," I said, sure I was blushing.

"Take as much time as you need to recover," Tap said, gently patting my shoulder before handing me an envelope.

"What's this?"

"Your pay, of course. I'll see you soon, Merry." He smiled, and walked away, not waiting for me to inspect it.

"Ready?" Seir asked.

I nodded, and as usual, he linked his arm with mine as we prepared to walk through the portal. Right before we stepped through, I peeked inside the envelope, panic fueled joy flooding my veins with electricity.

"That's too much," I breathed. Seir glanced at me with a concern that quickly morphed into amusement.

"What, that? Impossible. You've done a month's worth of work in only a few days. If anything, he should have tossed a few more notes in there as a bonus, especially given what a toll it's taken on you." He took the envelope from my hand and tucked it safely into my pocket, winked and pulled me through the doorway.

AFTER BARELY GETTING my tea steeped on my first rest day morning, there was a knock on my door. I'd been calculating how much I could spare to send back home and marveling at how it might feel to walk through the market without worrying about every single coin when I was interrupted.

"Merry? I know it's early, but I'm betting you'll like what I have to show you!" an excited Hailon called from the porch.

"Coming." I crossed the small distance quickly, trying not to spill my full cup as I walked.

I opened the door to find my friend looking over her shoulder at the large menagerie gathered around my yard.

"That's ... disturbing. I'm pretty sure some of them don't even live in this climate," she muttered, but her smile brightened as she turned back to face me. She lifted the basket cradled in her arms before pushing around the contents with a finger. "I left some at mine, but everything's here! Do you want to plant today?" Her gaze turned to the collection of wood carvings that had amassed over the week on my railing, a little twitch pulling at the corner of her mouth. There was now a raccoon, a fox, a doe, a fish, and a duck, along with the hawk and falcon. "Those are nice. House-warming gift?"

"Something like that." I leaned over and started poking around in the basket, impressed with the variety of things they'd been able to find. I'd thought I was making a wish list, but Grace had turned it into a proper order.

"You know Coltor fixed up my little horse for me, the one I've had forever? He's quite good at woodworking it seems."

"Mmm." I grunted a vague agreement. The carvings *were* quite good, but I didn't even have confirmation that they were from him, only an assumption. "And yes, we should get seeds for the squash and greens in the ground as soon as possible, otherwise it may frost too early for them to ripen."

"I thought so too. Seir is getting us some pots for the seedlings. I like the idea of being able to bring them inside if it's going to be cold. They need some time to grow before they go in the ground anyway."

I agreed wholeheartedly, and I went to change into my shabbiest clothes so we could get to work.

We started in the back of the cabin, Hailon following along and either copying my motions or awaiting instructions as she filled me in on what I'd missed while down in the library at the crossroads.

A headache started creeping in by the time we'd finished planting the first bed full of squash and assorted greens, and only got worse as we moved to the front beds where most of the animals still lingered.

"Hello," I greeted them all. Cautiously, I raised my eyes to glance around and got a strange muted barrage of greetings in return. *Hello. Help? Hear? Bond. Must pledge. Welcome. Friend!* No paralysis, though, which was nice. And the tone had changed a bit, like perhaps they were also offering help instead of simply asking for it.

I sectioned out the beds, roughly marking with a stick where I wanted which plants and left the little packets of seeds where they were meant to go. Between us, Hailon and I carved little trenches with our fingers and dropped in seeds before covering them up again. We had a good rhythm going when she finally spoke again.

"There are so many now," Hailon said reverently, her eyes trained on the family of quail nested up in some grass. Occasionally one of the chicks popped up and ran a few laps around the rest before cuddling back in. "Any new clues about what you're supposed to do for them?"

I explained to her what Tap had told me about the contracts, what little I was picking up when we spoke. "Hopefully there won't be so many soon." I needed to make a trip to see Ophelia to discuss the book she'd given me. I'd flipped through the whole thing, but it was like it was written in some kind of secret code. I couldn't make sense of hardly anything it said.

"Come on," Hailon said a bit later, clapping her hands together to free her fingers of some heavy soil. "Let's go to mine. Least I can do is fix you lunch before I make you help me with my beds too."

The animals cleared a gap for us to walk through, then followed us across the glade, my headache bad enough Hailon noticed I wasn't quite myself halfway through our sandwiches and brought me some medicine.

"Perhaps we should finish another day?"

"No," I refused. "I just need some more water, probably. I'll take a nap after we're done, it'll be fine." I was also fantasizing about a long soak in one of the hot springs. It seemed logical that doing that might relax me as well. I didn't know if it was the animals, the dust from the paperwork, or having been working so much, but I hadn't hurt like I was now, perhaps ever before.

"You're sure?" Hailon's eyebrows were pinched together with worry.

I put on my brightest smile, finished my last bite and got to my feet. "Absolutely. Let's get these seeds in the ground." The ache in my temples and down my neck raged as I nodded.

I'd never hoped for a medicine to work faster in my life.

CHAPTER 12
COLTOR

'D BECOME ONE of the things I hated most.

A coward.

My thoughts had become consumed by Merry. Even in my restless dreams she was there. Only stone sleep was a reprieve, and there was only so much of that I could do. I was plagued with figuring out how to prevent the fate I'd seen from happening, how to explain to her what I'd seen, and why I was acting the way I was. Even broaching a conversation, a casual one, felt like a ridiculously daunting task. Most of all, my thoughts circled around to apologizing to her. Both for behaving in such a manner and for being so temperamental in general.

In an attempt at regaining focus, I'd immersed myself in the carvings. At first, it was just a little hawk, something she might find cute. Leaving it on her porch had seemed clever at the time, but it too was a cowardly way of escaping a conversation. Now, she had as many wooden animals plaguing her cabin as real ones.

She'd seen them, I knew she had, because I'd been watching her from the shadows between the trees. But she hadn't touched any of them, nor taken them inside. I couldn't blame her for that reaction any more than I could keep myself from making more. She had every reason to refuse to accept them and I couldn't prevent my tendency to turn that rejection into a need to keep trying.

Then there were her trips through the portal to her new job. Hailon and I had crossed paths one morning and she'd explained with bright enthusiasm that Merry was working with Tap. It shouldn't have, but that too irritated me.

Emry, at least, had returned to work, no worse for wear, just in time for the cabins to be completed aside from the interiors. Somehow, despite the hammering going away, the glade had gotten louder—the wildlife had grown concerningly in number. My teeth ached regularly from being clenched together so tightly, and I constantly felt on the edge of a complete breakdown. I hated it.

Unable to settle down after my rounds, I went to leave another carving on the porch, expecting that Merry had gone to the crossroads for the day. Instead, I found Hailon and Merry cheerfully planting seeds. A rush of emotions passed through me, feet frozen on the path. As I watched them, my chest ached like I'd been the one to be impaled by a roof tile instead of Emry.

Tired of my own madness, I pocketed the wooden rabbit and used my wings to get me to the portal to avoid being seen by them. Feeling like there was a raging hornet's nest in my gut, as I crossed the grounds at d'Arcan, and carried myself straight to Ophelia's hut.

Her powerful wards weighed down on me like always, a sense of panic pressing in the moment I crossed into her part of the Dread Forest. The urge to turn back, to leave such a place, was insistent, but I knew it would pass.

A vision came across my mind so abruptly when I first touched down, I stumbled, falling to my knees in the dirt.

Ophelia, in her chair, her teacup shattered on the floor. This vision imparted the very insistent feeling that she was no longer in her physical body, that she'd abandoned this place for the next plane without so much as a farewell. I lurched to my feet and sprinted across the yard.

Heart pounding, I knocked on her door and waited. When no response came, I knocked again. Concern grew as I saw that the blooms in her flower boxes were wilting and there was a layer of dirt and leaves accumulating on her stoop. Despite the appearance of clutter inside, Ophelia was not one to let her home become unkempt. I'd quickly learned that everything in her little dwelling was stacked with intention, piled up in a precise order. She knew where everything was and why it was there, even if it made no sense to anyone else. Neglect and disorder were worrisome.

"Ophelia? Are you here?" I called, as if she would be anywhere else.

Fear gripped me for multiple reasons as I knocked on the door again. If I invited myself in, I could very abruptly end up in the afterlife. But if something was wrong with my kin, one of our elders in particular, and I just left ... I'd never be able to forgive myself.

I tested the knob, and to my surprise, it turned with ease. It occurred to me then that I had no idea whether or not Ophelia ever bolted her locks at all. Anyone brave enough to come into the Dread Forest and not run screaming from her heavy warding and march straight up to her door might actually deserve to meet Ophelia face to face. Not that they'd survive it necessarily, but they'd have earned it.

Bracing myself, I took a deep breath and pushed the heavy wooden door open.

Instead of the fresh-baked-bread smell that usually greeted me, or the heat from her oven, there was nothing but stale cool air and heavy silence.

"Ophelia?" I moved quickly through the kitchen to the living room, acid in my throat and a cold sweat prickling along my back. My eyes took in the shelves, the table, the stacks of books and papers. I went warm with relief as my eyes found her empty chair, nothing but the well-worn pillow and dented cushion right where it belonged.

Going into her bedroom felt like a violation, but I had no choice. I pushed the door open slightly, and a breath left me in a rush. She was tucked in tight under an old quilt, stone sleeping in the same position I imagined she'd take a regular nap in.

Relieved, I removed myself back to the main room and scribbled out a note for her, letting her know I'd checked on her and would likely be back to do so again.

I left the paper under the rabbit carving I still had tucked in my pocket on her coffee table, and fled the hut, taking flight as soon as possible to get out from under the oppressive wards.

As I made my way back toward Revalia, I calculated how many days it had been since I'd seen Ophelia last. If I had it right and she'd gone immediately to her rest that day, she'd been locked in stone sleep for five or six days. Most of us only did multiple days if there was an extreme case of exhaustion or injury. Ophelia was ancient, and I had no idea how frequently she might take a restorative stone sleep, but everything about this felt wrong somehow. I scratched at my arms, unable to shake the sensation of something crawling around under my skin, the prickle of warning that had never once been wrong needling at my senses.

I'D ENDED UP making a quick flight to the conclave to let Lovette know what I'd found at Ophelia's hut, as my father was at the council building instead of d'Arcan. My sister had given the same thoughtful silence and frown when I told her the number of days I suspected it had been since Ophelia went into her rest, but she promised to investigate where she could and let our father know if I didn't see him before she did.

Confident I'd adequately reported my concerns to those with much more ability to do something about it than I could, I portaled back to the glade. Weary to my bones, I shuffled along the path, preparing myself to be brave, to knock on Merry's door and look her in the face even if it meant she slammed it in mine.

Like the coward I was, I manufactured a way to delay such a meeting and decided to venture past the new construction by the hot springs pools first.

The construction noise was gone, but the steady hum that followed the wildlife around got louder as I approached the pools. One of the deer glanced up, and the birds scattered from the trees as I passed under the branches. There were now white foxes and hares I was sure had traveled from somewhere cold, like Ravenglen or Vincara. Strange deer with antlers unlike the type that was native here. The local wildlife had been bad enough, but now they were coming from elsewhere? I'd given up keeping track, as the numbers had grown so much in recent days, but I was doing my best to represent several of the new species with the carvings that kept my hands busy in the hours I couldn't find other distractions.

I was grumbling to myself about the invasion when it was suddenly as though I'd swallowed hot coals. My chest ached and burned, my ribs sore with every breath. I clutched at myself, palm rubbing along the muscles, the gesture useless in relieving the burn.

My eyes passed over the collection of animals scattered around, searching for the object of their infatuation.

Through the fur and the feathers, lying on the stones among the wild flowers growing through the cracks, was Merry. I choked on the air, a gruff gasp rumbling through my throat and panic flooding my veins with ice.

Her positioning, the way her hand lay limply on the stone ...

"Merry!" I shouted her name and lurched forward, the sound desperate as it reached my ears. The burn in my chest intensified as I grabbed at her wrist to check for a heartbeat.

She was bleary-eyed as she sat up violently, one arm swinging and the other dangling from my fingers. I was oddly relieved that at least she had some defensive instincts. The animals startled, several moving further away, feathers drifting on the breeze as she squinted and blinked, clearly trying to sort out what she was seeing. "Coltor?"

"What are you doing out here? Are you hurt?" My instincts screamed at me to grab her up, take her to her cabin, get her inside, and make her safe. I shook with the effort to contain that need as she ran a hand over her body, verifying she was in one piece.

"I'm fine. I ... fell asleep after sitting in the water for a while." Her hair was still damp now that I was looking, the color darker and her curls more pronounced.

She frowned, rubbing her free hand across her chest. Her eyes drifted from my face to my hand, and I released her. After a moment, I cautiously reached out to help her to her feet. Relief had washed away the bitter taste of fear, but I was still reeling. Twice in a day was too damn much for things like this. It was like the universe was testing me, having a laugh at my expense.

"Didn't mean to scare you," I grumbled.

She dusted off the back of her skirts with her hands. "Looks like I did that to you first, so we're even."

I nodded and we stood there for a long moment, not speaking, glancing around awkwardly.

"Listen, Merry, I—"

"Coltor about the—"

We both tried to speak at once, starting and stopping at the same time before she broke the tension altogether by laughing at me. She started toward her cabin, the animals scattering then forming a tight wall around her. I hesitated so long I was effectively blocked out.

She glanced over her shoulder. "Come on then. You can bring all those carvings inside for me, then apologize properly over a bite to eat." Merry stopped, finding me still standing where she'd left me, too stunned to move. "You *have* been practicing some kind of apology, haven't you?" the smirk on her mouth, the way her eyebrow lifted in challenge did something to every bit of my ability to think clearly as all the blood in my head fled south. Finally, I managed a nod. "Good." She spun, marching down the path with authority.

I ached for this woman.

After a long, noisy beat with animals of all kinds squawking and chattering around me, I made my body move and followed along behind her, a wholly different possible future, one that had nothing to do with my gift, playing behind my eyes.

CHAPTER 13
MERRY

THE DAFT MAN had hardly uttered a word since he'd called my name by the pools. There had been something in his voice, a particular kind of terror that I'd only heard once before. It made me shiver.

A few years back, my brother had climbed a tree every single adult in his life had told him explicitly *not* to climb. It was too tall with not enough branches at good distance for steps. He'd been challenged by a schoolmate to climb higher than anyone else had before, and like an idiot, he'd taken the bait. To his credit, he'd managed to accomplish his task, but the branch he'd ascended to wasn't sturdy enough to hold him.

My mother's scream as he tumbled to the unforgiving ground below still echoed in my ears. More than one broken bone was owed to that damned tree, including my brother's leg. It was thanks to Hailon that he'd been treated properly and could still walk.

I shook the memory and the guilt of not knowing how they were doing away as Coltor shrugged his large frame into my cabin. Somehow, he took up all the space in the open room. There was no escaping his woodsy scent, or how he somehow used up all the air. He somehow seemed even taller under a roof than he did out in the open. My face warmed as I stared at him, the way his eyes crawled along the little things I'd started collecting since I moved in echoing through my body like he was examining me with similar discernment.

"Where should I ..." He lifted his arms, the collection of carvings cradled between them.

"The fireplace is fine for now." His eyebrows shot up. "On the hearth, not actually in it. I promise I'm not going to use them for kindling," I reassured him.

I was rewarded with a view of his broad shoulders as he turned and squatted down to do as I asked, lining the little wooden animals up neatly across the stone hearth. He was wearing his hair mostly down for a change instead of braided, the long straight strands from the front pulled away from his face with a leather tie and the rest hanging down his back. As he turned the little wooden creations the way he wanted, I pulled together some food. I organized a plate with bread, cheese and sliced fruit, hoping it was enough to satisfy his hunger. I'd get back to cooking properly one of these days, but between Hailon providing half my meals and my days at the cross-roads, this was a much better match for my energy levels lately.

Coltor was glancing over at me as though waiting for an in-vitation as I set the board of snacks on the dining table. I said nothing, just gently waved a hand toward the food. He ducked his head in polite acceptance, plunking himself down in a chair that was two sizes too small for his body.

"I"—he twisted his fingers together, waiting for me to select what I wanted before he reached for a few things—"owe you an apology." His eyes flicked to mine, then back to his plate. "Several, most likely."

I took a slice of bread and spread a thick layer of some herby whipped goat cheese Hailon and I had found in the city on it, letting him stew while I chose my response. "What for?" I wanted to know if he understood exactly what he was apologizing about.

Coltor sighed, setting down the bread he'd taken before ever managing a bite. "Being … me, I suppose."

"What does that mean?" I frowned at him. I didn't appreciate his attitude much of the time, but he wasn't a bad man. It bothered me that he thought poorly of himself.

"I was alone out here for a very long time. Social graces and manners are not my strong suit."

I snorted. "It was not lack of manners that had you snapping at me over a garden tool." I shook my head and crunched into an apple slice before continuing. "Would you like to tell me what exactly had you so riled up over me making planting beds?"

His jaw and knuckles flexed in sync. "I don't know."

"You don't know?" This odd conversation felt no different than having to coax the truth out of my siblings when they'd done something they shouldn't have. "Is it that I was making changes when I'd only just arrived?"

"No." He fidgeted in his seat, trying to get comfortable, or perhaps unable to. "I don't care what you do with the yard. And gardens are an improvement. They'll be good for us all, provided you can keep the animals out of them."

"The animals won't be a problem." In fact, they'd already taken to eliminating any bugs threatening my sprouts, and I'd yet to see a weed. *Help*, indeed. "What, then?" I prompted, licking a stray dollop of the fluffy cheese from my thumb. His eyes tracked the movements and he swallowed, Adam's apple bobbing in his throat.

"I …" He sucked in a long, deep breath. "I was worried for you."

I rolled the words over in my head, making sure I had them right. "Worried?"

"Yes. That blade was very sharp. You could have been hurt."

"So you said. It's made that way on purpose, you know. A dull blade would be worse."

It was his turn to chuff, though the sound held little humor. "Oh, I know. All too well, I'm afraid. My sister is forge mistress, and I've trained with a sword since I was a youngling. I'm well educated on blades." The muscle in his jaw ticked again as he avoided my eye.

"Well, lucky for you I'm skilled with that kind of tool. Been gardening since I was a child myself, so I was never in any real danger." He nodded shallowly. "Have you been watching me?"

His hand rubbed across his chest, a grimace on his face like he was tasting acid. "Yes." My eyebrows jumped up. I hadn't expected him to be honest. "But not on purpose. Not ... really. Just to be sure you were safe. I only ever wanted to be sure you were safe." He sagged, a sadness crossing his face that had the tiny hairs on the back of my neck rising. The chair scraped the floor as he stood. "I should go."

"We're not finished talking yet though."

Coltor's mouth opened and closed again. "I'm sorry, Merry. I really should—"

"Coltor." I heaved a sigh, exhausted by the tension between us. "Sit down. Please." I tapped my fingertip on the tabletop with every syllable. Slowly, he sank back into his seat. "Thank you. Speaking of blades, care to explain the carvings?"

He shrugged, body slouched like he was trying to vanish into himself. "Something I do to keep my hands busy."

"They're lovely. Very detailed. You have a talent for it." He seemed more perplexed than anything else, a scowl drawing his mouth into a pout.

"I was ugly to you. I shouldn't have been, so I wanted to do something ... nice." His lips pursed again, and he took the opportunity to shove some cheese and a berry into his mouth.

"It's a sweet gesture, thank you." I stared at him until he continued.

"It ..." He stopped, clearing his throat. "It was out of line to speak to you that way. I shouldn't have looked in your windows, or come into your home without asking first, either. It's just, I ..." He shook his head. "Even if I did it for what I thought was a good reason, it was wrong, all of it."

"I appreciate that." His head bobbed, and we both ate a few bites, the silence heavy between us. "Do you want me to leave?" I asked, and his head snapped up, dark eyes wide. "Rylan offered an apartment at d'Arcan. Or I can return to Ophelia's. Am I unwelcome here?" My heart squeezed in my chest. I liked it here. The little cabin I couldn't help think of as mine, the peaceful glade, being close to my friend. It was a gift, and I wasn't ready to give it up.

"No." He shook his head vigorously. "You have every right to be here. You should stay."

"But you're not happy about it."

The corners of his mouth turned down, lines creasing the corners of his eyes. "It's not you."

"The animals then? I've got my own complaints about them, if we're being honest." Many, many complaints, most of which I'd found no resolution for yet.

"Them congregating here isn't your fault. No, there's no reason for you to leave, I swear it." I could see the words pained him, but he was being sincere.

"Then why do you look at me as though I'm personally responsible for the ills in your life?"

He frowned, then shifted around in the uncomfortable chair before getting to his feet. He wandered back to the fireplace, hand rubbing across his broad, muscular chest. I waited.

"I don't look at you like that."

"I disagree." I'd caught him several times, in fact, studying me like I was some kind of insect destroying a favored crop. As though if given enough time, he'd figure out a way to stamp me out of his life forever.

His mouth tightened. "I don't mean to. But if I do, it's not you. The glade has become very ... noisy."

Of all the things he could have said, that was not what I'd been expecting. "Sorry?"

He gestured with his hands, a grimace on his face. "The construction, the animals, the people. It makes it difficult to think. And people naturally want to talk, and I'm not so good with my words, as you well know. Or schooling my expression, clearly." He scowled as though picturing several transgressions. "They trample the flowers when they go off the path and don't take care of things like they should. They should respect it more because they don't live here, because it's not theirs, but they get careless sometimes. And it's all ..." His large arms flailed a bit, but he settled for gripping his hair for a brief moment, palms mostly covering his ears. "Loud."

"Oh." I understood Coltor much better in that moment, many missing pieces finally slotting into place.

"In truth, I didn't want you to move in here, not at first," he admitted, but quickly held up a hand, wide-eyed. The briefest ache of rejection stabbed through me. "But I didn't really want *anyone* here. Like I said, I'm used to being alone. I was, for a very long time. My isolation here came with its own problems, I recognize that. But I don't mind you here, Merry. I swear it. You're welcome in the glade for as long as you want to stay."

"Thank you." The sting faded as quickly as it had come.

He dropped his chin to his chest, rubbing his temples with his fingertips. "The noisiest part of all the construction is finished, and you're working with the crossroads demon about the animals. There are no plans to move anyone else in right away that I know of. I'll have some quiet again. It'll be alright."

A pang of guilt shot through me. I understood all too well how hard it was to adjust to so much change, the desire for some peace. A great many things had happened in his space after a long stretch by himself. It was no wonder he was short when dealing with others sometimes.

"That wasn't so painful, was it?" I teased gently, seeing that the huge man was still incredibly out of sorts by having such a conversation.

He scowled. "Guess not." I laughed, shocking him yet again. "What were you doing by the pools today? Why were you sleeping out on the stones?"

"I was worn out. The gardening, plus all the work I did at the crossroads." I shook my head. "I think it just caught up to me. I had a headache—"

"Do you need a remedy? I have some things."

I flushed hot at his abrupt, genuinely concerned offer. "No, I'm fine, thanks. I took something before we went to plant at Hailon's, and then after we were done, I soaked a bit. I didn't intend to nap, but I laid down on the warm stones to dry off and closed my eyes." His panicked tone, the terror on his face as he held my arm in his hand flashed through my mind. "Why were you so scared when you found me?"

He folded his arms over his chest, fingertips tapping on his upper arms. "Who said I was scared?"

I raised an eyebrow. "The tone of your voice when you called my name."

Irritation crept into his words. "Well, it's not every day I find a woman unconscious by the hot springs, is it?"

"I suppose not. For what it's worth, I appreciate your concern." I stood, and began to clear the table. "About the garden blade, my safety here alone, today. But I really can take care of myself, Coltor. I'm no youngling. Haven't been for a very long time."

"So you've said."

"Well, it's true."

A faint smile lifted the corner of his mouth. "Oh? How many harvests have you seen, Merry?"

I appreciated how he phrased the question but couldn't resist a tease. "Which one? Spring? Summer? Winter?"

He twitched a grin. "Lady's choice."

"Thirty-four. You?"

I was rewarded with a full, genuine smile. It stole my breath. He really was very, very handsome. High cheekbones, strong jawline. Expressive eyes and enviably long lashes. "One hundred and fifty-one."

I blinked. It shouldn't have been a surprise, but it still left me speechless. "Ah."

Coltor chuckled, the sound vibrating into my bones. He looked toward the ceiling and sighed. "I know you can care for yourself, Merry. You and Hailon remind me quite a lot of my sisters in that way. All the women I know are impossibly independent and terribly capable." His fisted hand rubbed lightly against his thigh. I couldn't help but laugh in response.

"Lucky you." He grunted. "Apology accepted." He was fidgeting still, looking unsettled. "Is there something else?"

"I ..." He shook his head, clearly at war with himself.

"You can tell me. I won't be upset."

"It's just that I ..." His face scrunched up. "Someone got hurt at the construction site. I had to take him to the conclave for healing."

"Oh! That's terrible. I hope everything's alright."

"He's fine." He nodded, but his jaw flexed. I could feel that wasn't all, but he wasn't talking, and I didn't know the best way to push. His voice was startling in its softness when he added, "Please be careful, Merry."

His dark eyes met mine and there was deep sorrow there that hit like a blow. "I will. I am." I dipped my head and added. "If it helps, I'm rarely alone. Never, actually, if you count the animals." This seemed to satisfy him, at least for now.

Coltor helped me finish cleaning up, and then I followed him out to my little porch. He'd spent all the words he had for the evening, it seemed.

As expected, the animals were all gathered around, doing their best to settle in for the night. There were even some species I hadn't seen anywhere outside the mountains back home. I made eye contact with several of the new ones, sharing a quick greeting.

Hello! Pledge bond? Help. Hear? Speak. Friend.

There was no sense of danger from any of them, just expectant attention, like they were trying to communicate something I clearly couldn't understand. By the time I got my eyes safely back on the dirt, my headache was back like it had never eased at all.

"I'd best get ready for my patrol," he said.

"Thank you for the carvings. And the apology." All my anger had gone, replaced by a deep want to comfort him, if only for a moment. He gave a single nod, and I raised myself on my toes, intending to kiss his cheek. Coltor startled, and the movement brought my mouth to his. Committed, I put my hand on his jaw to hold him in place. To my surprise, his massive palm came over mine, and his lips softened. The kiss was brief, but clearly rocked us both to the core.

When I pulled away, heart racing, Coltor blinked several times, then stepped down off the porch. He took a few steps, then turned back twice before managing to speak. "Pleasant evening to you, Merry," he said finally, striding off at a hasty pace down the path. His heavy steps caused several clusters of critters to startle.

"And to you," I muttered to myself with a smile, touching my tingling lips with my fingers. He was odd but not without his charms. I stayed on the porch, only turning to go inside once I couldn't see him anymore.

CHAPTER 14
COLTOR

I AVOIDED MERRY FOR the next few days, though I did leave some new carvings on her porch. The truth was, where she was concerned, I kept swinging between being stunned and ashamed. The opportunity to be honest with her about my vision had been right in front of me, and I'd been unable to force the words out despite her readily offering forgiveness for my other affronts. Then she'd kissed me and everything I knew had shifted, and the world had made sense for a moment.

The urge to continue checking in on her only intensified, my nerves extra frayed after finding her by the pools like I had. I felt like I might lose my sanity over the next several days as I tried to keep up with a change in her routine.

Seir started stopping by her cabin every morning. They'd say their greetings, and he'd take a crate full of paperwork and proceed to the portal. Merry had started staying behind. She'd drink a cup of tea while watering all her seedlings, then she'd vanish inside, new carving in hand.

This part pleased me far more than I wanted to admit.

In the evenings, as I prepared to set off for my rounds, I'd find her out with her watering can and often a few new visitors in the glow of the setting sun.

No matter the time of day, the sun caught her hair, sending off sparks. A halo of flames. She flitted around her gardens, always busy, constantly glowing. I couldn't shake the image of her as a firebird, especially when she put her arms out a certain way and a trick of the light would give her flaming wings.

It would have been foolish and an outright lie at this point to deny that I was taken by the stunning woman.

Still, I was braced for the worst, and my thoughts remained focused on her both asleep and awake. I didn't understand what it meant that my visions about Merry and Ophelia had manifested differently than I'd foreseen. While my vision about Ophelia had been wrong, she was still in stone sleep, which for all intents and purposes wasn't all that different than dead. I wasn't sure there were any of my kin who could pull her from it if that's what it came down to. I couldn't help but expect something else where Merry was concerned too.

On my way back from patrol near the end of the week, I found her on the path near the portal. The sun was high in the morning sky, hours past her normal plant-watering time. I'd stayed out longer than I normally did, some unusual activity in the doorways having kept me occupied past sunrise. It turned out to be nothing of concern, just a disturbance in the magic of the portal itself, but it had thrown my schedule off by several hours.

I approached her from the front, ensuring she could see me land and change from my slightly shifted stone kin body with wings to my human form.

She blinked. "That's quite a fascinating process." Her voice was low and breathy. The way she said it, the slow track of her eyes over my body lit my blood on fire.

"On your way to the crossroads? Don't you usually go with Seir?"

She shook her head. "No, I'm allergic to the dust or something there, so they've been bringing my work to my cabin instead."

"Oh. Revalia then? To the market? Or to see your horse? I could accompany you, if you like." I blushed as the offer tumbled off my lips. I'd made a visit of my own just the day before, but if she needed me to, I'd go back.

Greta had accepted the challenge of trying to craft an elixir that could limit the damage sustained by an injury, and Rylan, fascinated by the request, was also working on a similar charm that could be embedded into a stone or other trinket. Jacks had seemed unusually irritable as he paced the fence in the paddock, but I was not a horseman, and the groom had been caring for him.

Merry's eyes jerked to my face from where they'd been lingering around my shoulders and her cheeks turned pink. "Yes. No. I see Jacks in the afternoon usually. I'm going to Ophelia's. I'd be happy for your company if you'd like to come with me."

"You can't," I said, and Merry frowned. Her eyes were tired, glossy. Her hand idly rubbed at the muscles in her neck.

"Why not?"

"She's stone sleeping. Has been for quite some time."

"Oh." She frowned. "Is that unusual? To stone sleep for a long stretch?"

"It is. My kin and I are keeping an eye on her though." Between myself, my father, and my sisters, someone had checked once every day or so since I first found her. Absolutely nothing had changed, but Lovette seemed certain she was just resting.

Merry swallowed, both of us taking in the swath of wildlife that surrounded her at all times. I was becoming concerned about the resources for them in the glade. So far, they all seemed to be peacefully co-existing, but if they depleted what the area could offer, that surely couldn't last.

"Is she alright?" Merry asked, drawing my attention away from the animals.

"We don't know," I admitted. "She's one of the oldest of us. The rules are not the same."

Her face fell. "I hope she's okay."

"Me too."

We stood there a long moment, the urge to hold her nearly overwhelming me. "You seem tired. Are you ill?"

She touched her temple. "Just a headache."

"Another one?" After a brief hesitation, she nodded, but I could see she regretted the movement straightaway. "You should rest."

Merry closed her eyes and let out a long breath. "I really need to speak with Ophelia."

"Maybe someone else at the conclave can help?" I offered. "I could take you there. What did you need her for?" There was no escaping the sudden flush that lit up my whole body. I'd essentially offered to take her home, to introduce her to my whole extended family, and I hadn't even hesitated. The words had tumbled off my tongue like it was the most natural thing in the world. My pulse tripled as I tried to figure out what that meant.

"It's the book she gave me about hearing the animals, being a conduit. I can't make any sense of it." Her face dropped. "I thought by now, with the number of contracts I've sorted, the animals would be leaving in droves. Some have, but there are more. Always more." The strain in her face was highlighted by the shadows cast when she turned her head. I ached to reach for her.

"Perhaps someone at d'Arcan then?"

She shook her head, then winced, a hand flying to her forehead. "Hailon and I went the other day. Whatever language or encoding it's in, it's not known to have origins with the stone kin, demons, witches, or fae. Tap tried to read it as well, as he's the keeper of the contracts, and even he was perplexed. Ophelia had made it seem like it was a simple little guidebook. I'm so confused. This feels like some kind of test, and I'm failing miserably." She sighed. "Could you please let me know when she's ready for visitors again?"

"Of course."

"Thanks." Merry turned back down the path, steps intentionally slow, soft.

My chest ached. Even *walking* hurt her.

"Should I fetch Hailon for you?"

Her curls bobbed as she shook her head, one hand twisting the bracelet on her wrist around and around. "She's in the city today."

I'd had enough. *I* was here. *I* could help.

"I'll see you home. They should not have left you like this." I softened my tone. "I will not leave you like this."

"I'm fi—" I stepped in front of her and scooped her up, then let out my wings so I could glide us back to her cabin. She'd squeaked but didn't fight to be let down. Instead, she grabbed on tight, arms lashed around my neck and legs held snugly in the bend of my arm. The close contact had my whole body alight. I breathed her in, the scent of sunshine and berries flooding my senses. Something under my ribs gave a wild throb, and I had to cover my gasp with a grunt.

"Don't lie to me. You're not fine, Merry."

I got her into the cabin in short order, settling her comfortably on the sofa. I fetched a glass of water from her kitchen and offered it to her with some of the shimmery elixir that was sitting by the sink. Greta's work, by the looks of it.

"This is all very sweet but completely unnecessary, Coltor. Thank you though. And I can't take any more of that until later, I had some before I left for the portal." Her praise sent a bright thrill through me. "It should start working soon, honestly. I'll be alright. I promise to rest."

"Drink." Her eyebrow raised, but she did as I asked. I paced, arms crossed as she sipped. "How bad?"

"How bad what?"

"The headache. How bad is it? How long has it been going on like this? Do you need a healer?"

"Hailon has checked me over and everyone else at d'Arcan as well. I'm just ... tired. I think the animals are the cause, if I'm honest. Blocking them out takes a special kind of effort I don't know how to control. It's like I'm doing it naturally, but the more of them there are, the more it's taking out of me. Greta made me that elixir, and Rylan said he'd work on a trinket for me, but that might take a while. Ophelia said eating something sweet would help, but I'm tired of honey and jam."

I could only grunt. That was not a resolution. She needed Ophelia.

Unfortunately for us both, so did I.

I blew out a rough breath and made for the door. "Stay put." The command indulged the growing part of me that felt driven to hide her away from the rest of the world, to protect her from it. That part of me was far larger than I wanted to admit and was refusing to be ignored.

"I may go to bed instead, or soak in the tub. Is that alright?" She raised an eyebrow, sarcasm heavy. She'd do what she pleased, regardless of what I asked of her, we both knew that.

"If you insist. But stay inside. Please. I'll be back very soon. I'm going to get a few things from my hut." Her eyebrows knitted, but she agreed with the slightest inclination of her head.

That was agreement enough for me. I drove my wings hard toward the ground the second I was on the outside of her door so no time would be wasted. I had several stone kin remedies stashed away in a cabinet, plus some old recipes that the aunts and my mother had sworn by for situations like this.

Hopefully that would be enough for now.

"WHAT'S ALL THAT?" Merry asked still on the sofa as I set several bottles, some food and a couple of books on her table a short time later.

"I thought we might try a few things that work for stone kin, if that's okay."

The corner of her mouth twitched. "Alright."

I oriented myself in her kitchen, starting a pot of water on the stove. I sliced up some oranges and added a couple of cinnamon sticks. Once it was heated and started to perfume the air, I put it on a very low flame. Outside, I used the water pump to fill one of her clean, shallow buckets with cold water.

Things long since forgotten from watching my father help my mother when she got her blinding headaches started coming back. I wondered what else I'd forgotten about her, how similar our gifts might be.

"This is going to seem a little strange, but will you trust me?" I asked her. She eyed the bucket, which I set down on the floor near her feet on a towel.

"I don't see the harm. For my feet?" I nodded. She tilted her head to the side but sank her delicate little feet in to above the ankles. "Freezing," she said through clenched teeth. "What does this do?"

"Helps," I answered, because honestly, I wasn't sure exactly, but it was a technique that stone kin used often for sore heads. "Can I touch your neck and shoulders?"

"Yes."

I adjusted the direction she was sitting a bit and settled on my knees behind the sofa. She pulled her long hair over one shoulder, twisting it so it was out of the way. After taking a deep breath to settle the flutter in my chest, I reached out and pressed my thumbs into the tense muscles on either side of her spine. I massaged along the column of her neck, then down into the bunched knots along her shoulders. She made small noises of distress when I hit the most tender places but began to relax after a few minutes, her smooth skin pliable under my heavy hands.

"Any better?" I asked, and her head bobbed lightly.

"Yes, thank you. Can I take my feet out of the water now? My toes are starting to wrinkle."

"Here." I went back around in front of her and knelt again as I moved the bucket off to the side and used the towel to dry her feet off. Then I turned her so she was lying on the sofa, well supported by pillows, and covered her with the blanket she kept there.

Her eyes were wide, the pupils large, and her cheeks pink as she looked at me like she'd never seen me before. There was surprise there but also trust. My chest burned, heart thumping so hard under my ribs I was breathless.

"Try to rest."

"I don't like this," she said, my heart kicking into double-time when I saw the shimmer of tears in her eyes.

"I'm sorry. I'll go. I just thought—"

"Not you, Coltor. This is actually really nice. I'm usually the one doing the caretaking, so this is new for me, but I don't mind. You're being very kind."

"The simmer pot then? Some people don't take to cinnamon."

She barked a short laugh, then reached out to catch my hand as I turned to go into the kitchen. "Will you sit for a moment?"

I could hardly breathe, and my chest felt like it was caught in a vice. "Of course." I settled myself carefully onto the low table in front of the sofa.

She held my hand in both of hers, examining it closely. I suppressed a shiver as she traced along the lines in my palm with her fingertip, then measured the size of her hand against mine, silent the whole while. I tried to focus on her bracelet instead of the furious rush of blood pounding through my body. It was braided hair of some kind, with a reddish stone woven in. It was clearly well loved, worn and fraying a bit near the clasp. It looked like her habit of turning around her wrist had irritated her skin.

Abruptly, she met my eye and stopped her gentle touch. Without thinking, I drew her hand to my face and kissed her palm.

"Oh." The word came out on a soft breath, but she didn't pull away. I guided her hand to my cheek and closed my eyes for a moment. Her skin was warm and soft, and she smelled downright edible. If I focused, I could hear her pulse throbbing, smell the slightest tang of iron on her skin. I brushed my mouth along her wrist as I gave her arm back.

I wanted nothing more than for her to continue exploring me at her leisure, but she tucked her arms under the blanket. I shifted around, not wanting her to see the effect her simple touch had had on me.

"I don't like feeling helpless," she said after a heavy pause, reminding me of what she'd said earlier. "I'm perfectly capable of taking care of myself. Jacks. My mother, even, and my siblings. I've done it all, for a long time."

"You're very strong, Merry."

"I am," she agreed with a nod. "What is it about this place that makes me feel both like I'm finally where I should be and completely out of my depth all at the same time, then? I have everything I could ever want. A house to myself, a job I enjoy that also pays well. Friends. But I can't figure out what those animals want from me. Why I feel this ..." Her hands fluttered under the blanket, but she never located a word for whatever she was trying to describe. She sniffled while looking me in the eyes, and I nearly lost it. "I also really hate crying." She pressed her hands to her face, trying to stop the tears, but it was no use.

Everything in my body screamed, wanting to comfort her as they dampened her cheeks. Instead, I sat there like an idiot, panicking. Finally, I reached out awkwardly. Resting my hand over hers somehow ended up with our fingers twined together.

"Can I tell you a secret?" I asked. My pulse throbbed in my throat, the stress of being open with someone, especially her, sent my heart pounding. But I thought we both needed this. She turned her head to face me and nodded, scrubbing her tears away. "I feel like that too, most of the time."

"You do?"

"Of course. This is my place. It's become my home even though it was only ever meant to be a temporary post. It's very confusing, how I feel about the glade. I wanted nothing more than time away until Seir arrived, but, if given a choice I would remain here always. I do my patrol, maintain the doorways, reinforce the wards." I shrugged. "It's a routine I enjoy, though it can get a bit monotonous when things go right and everyone stays away like they should. The magic here ... it's old, alive. Centuries have come and gone, nearly all that time without it being managed so carefully. I often wonder if I'm making any difference at all or if I'm just fooling myself that I'm being useful." She gave a weak smile. "And for the record, I also hate when you cry."

She stared at me in such a way, for so long, I was certain my whole face was red. Then she laughed, free and easy like a weight had been lifted from her. The sound tripped down my spine and sent a sparkling sensation through my veins. "Thank you, Coltor." Even the way she said my name was a novel treat, like the taste of it in her mouth was something special.

"You're welcome, Merry." I pulled on every ounce of bravery I had and kissed her forehead. The soft tilt of a smile, the sigh she exhaled, all the tiny ways she accepted the affection put lightning in my veins.

Her eyes finally drifted closed, the elixir perhaps beginning to work along with the remedies I'd performed. After watching the slow rise and fall of her breaths for an embarrassing amount of time, I snuck my hand out of her grasp and went outside as quietly as I could. The animals perked their heads at me but made no other effort to move. I was not gifted with mind speech and heard nothing but the sounds of them chattering to themselves and moving around in the grass.

"You're making her unwell. She can't help you if she's sick. Find someone else to speak with. Move along. Understood?"

There was a shuffle but no exodus.

Frustrated but determined to be useful, I went back inside and started preparing her a soup that always made me feel better.

CHAPTER 15
MERRY

EVERYTHING HAD CHANGED between Coltor and I. We'd shared little pieces of our souls, made gestures that couldn't be taken back.

After I'd woken from my nap, he fed me some incredible soup, then rubbed an aromatic oil on my temples. He insisted on working out the tension in my shoulders again, a cool towel against my neck and my feet back in an icy bucket. He stayed until it was time to leave for his patrol and looked as though he regretted having to go. He was quiet, but it was a soft silence, not one borne of frustration like I had seen from him before. Conversation was sparse, but his hulking presence was a comfort, the low timbre of his voice soothing.

Now that I knew where his anger had been rooted, I could see it for what it was. Overwhelm. Concern. Strain. I would have bet anything that taking care of me was a balm on those raw emotions. In fact, I understood that more than most.

He'd hesitated to leave that evening, his big shoulders taking up my whole doorway, so I'd put him out of his misery and kissed him. It seemed so silly, but his hesitant-turned-wholly-enthusiastic kisses revealed that all the others I'd had before were lacking in every way. Coltor was all-in when he wanted something, and by the way he wrapped his body around me, the way his mouth fed upon mine, there was no question that I was undeniably *wanted*.

I tried to ignore how terribly empty my little cabin had felt since he'd left, but it was impossible. There was too much space now, too much air. And I couldn't help but think of how gently he'd cared for me every time I saw the little family of carvings on my hearth. For all his faults, Coltor was inescapably a good man.

And the truth was I wanted him too. More than I thought was possible to crave another person. I had no idea how we'd arrived at this place, but there was nowhere else I'd choose to be.

THANKS TO HIS remedies and a good night's sleep, I felt better than I had in days. Head clear and ready to make a trip to the markets for myself, I prepared for a day out of my cabin and away from the contracts I was spending my days working through.

Seir and Tap, apologetic over the omitted information about the time difference and concerned that I'd worked myself too hard in addition to the concern about the dust allergy, had set up a system so I didn't have to go to the crossroads unless I really wanted to. Seir delivered a crate or two of new contracts in the evening and would stop by to pick up any completed ones in the morning on his way out. I was appreciative but hoped to return, if only occasionally, soon. Some animals had moved along after the first crates had gone back to Tap with Seir, but it was a disappointing few. The ones that continued to gather seemed restless, as well, like they were waiting for instructions or permission to do something. The dozens and dozens of expectant eyes watching me had me constantly tense. I was beginning to feel quite helpless about it all.

I stepped through the doorway, the familiar twisting sensation the least of my concerns. As I was spat out on the grounds of d'Arcan, it felt as though my head might split in two. I hit my knees and stayed there a moment, focusing on my breathing.

"Merry?" As I regained my feet, temples throbbing, Grace's voice came to me as if I were underwater. I could hear Jacks making a racket from across the yard and glimpsed him rearing up on his hind legs, kicking and generally making a huge fuss.

"Is Jacks alright?"

"She's tripped through a portal and is asking about the horse," Grace muttered, shaking her head. "I can appreciate that, honestly, but let's worry about you, yes? Are *you* alright?"

I forced a smile over the pain. "I'm fine. Just a little clumsy."

Her sidelong look told me she didn't entirely believe that, but she didn't press. "Well. What can we do for you today?"

"I need to send something to my family. Can you tell me the best way to arrange that?"

Her whole face lit up and she led me inside. "Of course, my dear. Come with me. We'll need to speak with the headmaster. Rylan?" she called.

"Yes?" He turned from where he was seated at the new family dining table as Grace hauled me into the dining room.

"Merry needs to send a package."

"An envelope," I explained. "But it's money, so I wasn't sure if there was a special way?"

"Ah. I've got just the thing." His smile was broad as he got to his feet and took us down the hall.

Rylan's massive black owl was perched on a tall stand near a person-sized hearth in a mostly empty classroom. Hearing us, he perked, head swiveling as he took us all in. I focused, prepared to hear him speak, but heard nothing.

"Archimedes enjoys a mission now and then. What do you say, care to take on a courier job?"

"I'd be happy to pay." I addressed both the owl and the mage and was amused to get a similar expression of interest from them both.

"He does love a good vole or rat."

"Anything you like, I'll be happy to get it." I cringed, but Rylan winked in a way that reassured me I would not be personally responsible for obtaining the rodents.

Archimedes stuck one of his legs out, talons open like he was requesting the item. "Do you have the envelope?" Rylan asked.

"Oh, of course." I dug it out of my pocket and handed it to Rylan, who passed it to Archimedes.

"Where is he going, exactly?"

The bird looked directly at me, his golden gaze intelligent and intense. I was proud that I managed not to look away and pleased his eyes didn't paralyze me. "Take it to the big market off the main street in Ravenglen, if you please. They'll get it to my mother. Her name is on the envelope and there's a letter inside."

Archimedes bobbed his head. It was then I heard a faint voice. *Help friend. Journey. Treat.* Then with a powerful flap, he flew out the window Rylan had crossed the room and opened.

"Is there anything else we can do for you today?"

"No, thank you very much."

"Anytime, Merry." Rylan gave a graceful bow, and I did a terrible imitation of a curtsy.

After allowing Grace to care for me with tea and honey cakes, I went to the paddock to see Jacks, who thankfully had calmed quite a bit. I fed him an apple and some carrots from the bucket near the gate, and he mouthed at my bracelet while I scratched his nose.

"I won't be back for a few days," I told him, resting my aching head against his. "I'm not feeling very well. You behave, alright?" Jacks looked at me in a way that had me convinced he understood, and I fought back tears as I threw my arms around his neck. "I bet if you could, you'd help me figure out what I'm supposed to be doing." He nickered gently, and I gave him a squeeze. "Maybe one day you can join me in the glade. Can horses use portals?" I tilted my head, and he snorted, but I was unsure if that was a yes or no. "Long way around perhaps, then. No matter. For now, stay here and get some pampering, yes? I'll come see you as soon as I can."

I walked away before I got too worked up and forced myself back to go back to the glade, worried I'd lied to Jacks for the first time ever as the portal split my head wide open before it spat me back out.

I DRAGGED MYSELF back to my cabin and slept for nearly a whole day. I felt slightly better upon waking again, but the persistent banging in my skull remained.

Even if I didn't see Coltor, there were new carvings waiting for me on the porch almost every morning. The variety of beasts on my hearth had grown nearly as vast as the actual animals still hanging around. He'd even made me a squirrel.

Unable to focus on the writing in the contracts, I took the little book Ophelia had given me and sat on the porch steps. I turned several pages, finding a word here or a phrase there that made sense, but not much else, just like every time before. Frustrated, I kept flipping while walking the garden beds, encouraging the little plants to grow with some gentle leaf pruning.

I looked around at the closest animals. "Thank you for taking care of the bugs and weeds. That's very helpful." I wasn't sure where it came from, but I did hear a faint response. *Welcome. Friend. Help. Pledge now?*

There was some gentle stirring as I started off toward Hailon's, but they followed at a respectful distance instead of crowding me along the path. About the time I crossed by the hot springs, I realized the words on the page in front of me were easily understandable.

I stopped walking, stunned by what I was seeing.

The words were suddenly clear, each and every one. I turned the pages again and again, finding the same. As I skimmed through a lesson on interspecies communication and went to turn the page, I stopped short. My wrist was bare.

I spun around, looking at the ground, wondering how long my bracelet had been gone. "No. No, no. It can't be." The sound in my head narrowed to a muted hum as panic sank in. My father's stone. One of the only things I had left of him. After he'd been missing long enough to be presumed dead in the mine collapse, my mother had fallen completely apart, and she'd never been able to put herself back together. I missed him terribly; he was the light in our tiny family of three. I hadn't been without my bracelet since it had been passed along to me.

I dropped the book as I went to my knees, sifting through the grass and weeds with my fingers, sobs working their way into my chest.

"Help me, please!" I cried. "Find my bracelet. It has to be here somewhere."

Help! Friend, help! Look!

Several animals sprang to action, rummaging in the foliage and soil with me. I crawled around in a blind panic for what seemed like an eternity, but still came up empty-handed.

Hands pressed over my eyes, I cried in earnest, the heavy emotion making my headache worse. Once I was finally wrung out, I looked around to realize the whole glade seemed far quieter than it should.

"What ...?"

The herds and flocks had hemmed me in—a wall of creatures all around me, a wide shadow covered the ground where the birds hovered in the sky over my head. They had never once felt threatening. Never moved in a way that seemed anything other than curious, patient. But they were too close, too quiet. I was more raw than normal, so their presence, their sorrow for my sadness felt heavy.

I glanced around, throat dry. I held my hands out as I slowly got to my feet. "Thank you for helping me search. I wish I knew what you wanted, I feel terrible I can't help you."

As the fog of my panic cleared, everything went from too quiet to too loud. It was like I'd had my ears stuffed with cotton, and I'd finally taken it out. The world around me exploded with violent noise and frantic movement. Heavy wings beat a brutal tattoo on the air; all of the normally cute little squeaks and grunts stabbed at my ears like screams. I was paralyzed by dozens of sets of eyes locking onto mine at the same time, the sound of my racing heartbeat throbbing in my ears. I fell to my knees, pain blossoming as I hit the stones.

I pressed my hands over my ears and squeezed my eyes closed. I might have screamed but couldn't hear myself.

Friend! Listen. Welcome! Blessings, Keeper! Help, friend! Ceremony soon? Sorceress, friend! Help too? Celebrate! Happy! Hear us, friend? Speak now, friend? Welcome! Hear? Accept? Friend! Speak? Loyal, friend. Hello! Accept pledge. Excitement, friend. Welcome, Keeper! Hear, friend? Speak, friend? Contract? Beautiful, friend!

"Please." The word escaped me as a whisper, nothing more than a puff of air against the gale assaulting my senses. They were not trying to hurt me, but some kind of veil had been lifted, and everything was rushing in at once. "One at a time. Please, slow down, I can't ... It's too much."

Their voices piled one on top of another in my head, whispers and shouts and everything in between. There was joy, excitement, urgency, all mashed together in a torrent of sound.

I could feel the edges of my sanity fraying away, and it was almost a relief. Because if I wasn't sane anymore, I wouldn't care a whit about what was happening. It would all be fine again on the other side of madness. They crept closer as I curled into myself.

I could feel their concern, that they'd noticed it was more than I could bear, but it was too late.

Help? Unwell? Sorry, friend. Help! Speak now, friend? Danger? No hurt!

The mind fracturing is an odd sensation. Warm, somehow. Even my awareness of what was happening didn't overwhelm the feeling of peace as the cacophony in my head lightened to a low hum. Eventually there was just white noise, like I was trapped with my head under a waterfall. I couldn't see, couldn't move.

Then, darkness came.

COLTOR'S BOOMING VOICE cut through the black space in my head.

"Off with you! Leave her be! Shoo! Go on! AWAY, THE LOT OF YOU!" The ground trembled as he loosed a monstrous roar, and a gust of wind blew across me as he beat his massive wings. There was a brief burst of animal chatter, noises of surprise and fear, then the flap of feathers and clop of hooves as they left. Many of the creatures had pressed against my body, trying to help restore me in their own way, but I didn't blame them for fleeing. There was no way for me to explain what had happened at the moment.

"Merry?" The tremor in his voice echoed through my chest, his fear palpable. "Merry!" His fingertips trembled, but they were warm as they pressed against the side of my throat. "Thank the saints."

I couldn't make my muscles relax. My eyes were closed, and the heavy lids wouldn't budge. My body had curled into as small a ball as it could manage, a defense against the onslaught of sound from the creatures that had swarmed around me. By the time they'd realized it was too much and settled down, I was frozen in that position.

"I've got you. You're alright."

I nodded—or tried to. Nothing seemed to work right. I was present in my own head, but I felt oddly untethered from my body.

Coltor's warmth surrounded me, one arm under my legs, the other tight around my back. I breathed him in, reveling in warm earth and woodsmoke.

His low voice rumbled through me. "You're not allowed to go yet, little firebird. I've only just found you." My heart did that funny beat again, too fast, like it was skipping, then squeezed in my chest. The sensation was unnerving, even in my current state.

He crossed the glade smoothly, like his feet weren't touching the ground. He avoided jostling me, but his large frame moved quickly. It occurred to me belatedly that he'd likely used his wings.

I was finally able to force my eyes open as we neared my cabin. Sensation was returning to my body, but very faintly, like a little needle sting. My fingers and toes were still unresponsive to my demands to wiggle, and my extremities felt like they were buried under heaps of wet soil.

"The wards will be a little better there. And I have my supplies." He muttered the words to himself as much as me as he continued past my cabin toward his.

Once inside, he set me carefully on the plush chair in the living room. He knelt down, a warm palm on either side of my face, his dark eyes rounded with concern. I realized then that my gaze wasn't following him when he moved, though my eyes blinked at regular intervals. I was truly trapped inside myself, not in control at all. It should have worried me, but I was floating somewhere above such inconvenient emotions.

"You're still in there, aren't you, Merry?"

I tried to signal to my body that my head should nod or that my eyes should blink—*anything* to show that I'd heard his question. But nothing happened.

"Not dead, but not alive either. Useless, cursed gift." It sounded almost like an accusation, but it didn't feel like it was aimed at me.

Coltor stuffed pillows around me so I couldn't slouch or tip out of the seat, then crossed the handful of steps into his tiny kitchen.

Cabinet doors opened and closed as his muttering devolved into colorful swearing.

"I need you to drink this. I got it from Greta, so it's as safe as any magical elixir can be. It should help." I couldn't do any kind of assisting, so Coltor tilted my head back, parted my lips and poured some of the contents from a vial of pink, shimmery liquid into my mouth. His thumb massaged my throat so that it would go down properly.

It struck me then how truly precarious my situation was. If such a thing had happened anywhere else, I'd have been in serious trouble.

He frowned but rose to dispose of the dishes. I could only stare at the wall as he moved around me, grumbling.

"What do I do? Take her with me to the demons? Go to Lovette?" I could hear the splash of water, the clank of dishes in a sink. "The elixir should work soon, and resting is probably safe." He returned to my side. "Tell me what to do, Merry. Yell at me. Cry. Anything."

I didn't feel particularly unwell, disconnection between my mind and body aside. I didn't know what a healer could do that whatever was in that elixir couldn't. Not that I could tell him so.

"I can't leave you like this. You need to be seen by someone." He stood, took two steps, then stopped again. "But I'm not sure it's best for you to portal right now." He growled. "What do I *do*?"

After a moment's hesitation, he bent and scooped me into his arms, and there was sky above me again. I watched over his shoulder as his wings deployed, and he carried us quickly to Seir and Hailon's cabin.

"Coltor?" Seir's tone held a note of urgency.

"I need your help." The desperation in Coltor's voice broke my heart. I couldn't even hold onto him as he carried me.

"Of course, come in."

Hailon's voice came from the other side of the cabin. "What's happened?"

"I found her by the pools. The animals, they were all around her. She was curled up, like she was protecting herself." He set me on their sofa, and Hailon came to kneel in front of me, her eyes full of concern. She snapped her fingers, waved her hand. I blinked, but not because I was intentionally responding.

I could hear the animals still, quiet now, worried and apologetic. But there was no way for me to tell them that the creatures hadn't intentionally harmed me.

"Seir? Can you—"

"I'll get the mirror."

My body started to feel warm, tingly. It wasn't unlike how I'd felt one Yule after enjoying far too much spiced cider the Mullvaney twins had spiked with their father's corn liquor. I lay there on the plush sofa, melting into the cushions as the elixir began to work, their voices blending together into a soft, familiar noise.

I floated back into consciousness over several brief intervals, never long enough to truly grasp onto how much time might have passed. Once, there'd been a very concerned blonde woman staring into my face and gently prodding at my limbs. Another time, I could hear both Rylan and Vassago, but I got the impression they were not actually in the room. Then, I heard Greta, but the same odd distant echo was there. Nobody seemed overly panicked, and that was oddly reassuring. I still controlled no part of myself, but it was warm and cozy in the little cocoon I was in, so I didn't care.

The next time I woke, it was to the sound of furniture scraping the floor. The woodsy smell of Coltor was heavy in the air.

"We'll fix it," he promised on a whisper. "You're going to be alright." He picked me up as though I weighed nothing and carried me a few steps, then laid me on a bed.

Coltor maneuvered me under the blankets and tucked me in tight before settling in behind me. I was immersed in the scent of woodsmoke and warm earth, his essence all around me.

I begged my eyes to open, if only for a moment, and was granted a couple of seconds to orient myself. I was next to and facing a wall, and I suspected that the bed was the furniture I'd heard being shifted around. It was thoughtful, honestly. While I wasn't normally one to roll off the side of a bed, as I had no control to speak of, I supposed it was a possibility.

His palm wrapped around my neck, his fingertips resting over where he could feel my heartbeat. Normally, someone's hand on my throat might have made me feel either murderous or like an overheated puddle in their hands. This, however, was a sweet gesture of concern.

My eyes slid closed, and I settled in, comfortable as the darkness took me again.

CHAPTER 16
COLTOR

OPHELIA HAD TOLD me that I would understand, that I would figure things out. She hadn't been wrong—clarity had hit me square in the chest, just not at all in the way I expected.

My gift was mostly a mystery still, as were the animals invading the glade. But Merry? I understood clearly now why I couldn't get a handle on my thoughts or feelings where she was involved. Why I wanted to consume her.

Merry was mine. My *mate*.

Such a gift was not something to scoff at, no matter how ill-timed it might seem, and it seemed terribly obvious once the realization struck me. I'd stood there, heel of my palm pressed into my chest and stared into the wall for a worrisome number of minutes once I'd finally figured out the truth.

So now I had two significant things to explain to Merry, and I didn't even know if she was still fully present behind those pretty brown eyes.

Gratitude had me steeped in emotion as I lay there in the dark, listening to Merry's soft breathing. Nobody had hesitated when I reached out for help. Seir had used that fascinating little mirror to contact his brothers, and before I knew what was happening, I was talking to them about the animals' behavior, how I'd found her near the pools. Then Greta had appeared in the glass to speak to me about an elixir, and Lovette had arrived in person to examine Merry alongside Hailon.

For once, I welcomed the noise. It brought relief. It meant I was not alone in this, and Merry would be well cared for.

On his way to take my post for the night, my father had gone to check on Ophelia. He reported that when he was leaving d'Arcan, Jacks had jumped the paddock fence. The horse followed him all the way through the city and into the Dread Forest. He was currently stationed outside Ophelia's hut.

"Demanded the colored glass window be opened, as well as the one in her room," he'd reported with a grin as we discussed my nightly route. "At least she'll have company when she wakes up."

I'd slept for a while, unreasonably comfortable next to Merry. When I woke, she'd rolled to her back, by all appearances resting peacefully. As she hadn't seemed able to move at all since I found her, this felt positive. I tried to settle down again, sure the next several days would be trying, but it was as though I'd grabbed onto a lightning bolt and the power was still lingering in my veins. I was raw, anxious.

I refused to leave Merry alone, but there was not enough space inside my little hut for the energy I had coursing through me. I slid off the bed carefully, so as not to disturb her, and went outside. The cool night air helped a bit as I dragged several deep breaths into my lungs. Then the creatures began to raise their heads, glowing eyes blinking at me from the darkness.

"You," I groused. "You did this. This is your fault." Several of the smaller animals ducked their heads as though they knew exactly what I was saying. "What is it that you want from her? Can't you go to someone else?" I could only growl to myself as they kept their silence. I walked over to my pile of carving wood and made a few selections, then sat on the steps to work.

As I scraped shavings into the dirt, creatures began cautiously approaching. A rabbit left a berry near my boot, a raccoon a half-eaten apple. Soon I had a small pile that included nuts and stones. There was even a coin from one of the birds.

"An apology, then?" I asked, their body language and gesture clear. Heads ducked and they settled in quietly while I continued to work.

By the time my father appeared at dawn, I'd finished a decent rendering of a spring star flower and had started the form of a bear, all while checking on Merry periodically and starting a stew for later. Anything to keep myself distracted, busy.

"Your post is enviable, son." My father wore a broad smile as he approached. "I don't think I've had such a nice night flight in quite some time."

"I enjoy it, mostly."

He glanced at the door. "Any change?"

"No." To my disappointment, Merry remained how I'd left her, breathing steadily, eyes closed.

"Should I send someone to relieve you? Give you a chance to rest?" His eyebrow raised, as though he'd already predicted my response.

"I'm fine."

My father nodded, glancing around at the animals who had dispersed a bit, and the pile of offerings.

"That's friendly," he muttered, nudging one of the stones with his toe. "Greta was working on medicines when I left, and Imogen was going to check on Ophelia today. Shall I come back tonight?"

I hesitated, deep guilt for not doing my own job, for interrupting the routines of everyone around me setting in. But I wasn't leaving her side, so there wasn't another choice.

"If you don't mind."

"Of course."

"I've got stew on," I offered after a painfully long silence. I got to my feet, but he just shook his head.

"I'll pass for now but appreciate the offer. I'm headed back to d'Arcan. Grace will likely have a meal ready and a list of chores for me to accomplish before I get a chance to sleep." The broad grin on his face told me he did not find any of this to be a hardship.

"Thank you, Father."

He bowed, then pulled me in for a hug that made me feel as though I were a child again despite the fact that I was as tall as him. "Anytime, my son. Anytime." His eyes met mine, the compassion and sincerity there battering at my already raw emotions.

It occurred to me then that Grace was similar in many ways to Merry, and my father might have some insight he could share with me. He'd been blessed with her as a second mate many long years after my mother had died in battle and returned to the stones. I hadn't spent much time with Grace, being as I existed mainly here in the glade, but I liked her well enough. She ran the inner workings of d'Arcan with a firm hand and was good for him. They were well matched.

I must have hesitated too long, because he asked, "Is there something else?" My mouth opened, but my scrambled thoughts were slow to formulate into words. "Mmm, I see." My father sighed, clapped me on the shoulder, leaving his hand there. "Indigestion?"

Confused, I frowned and stared at him. "Sorry?"

"Do you find yourself with unexplained indigestion? A burn, just here." He put a fist to his chest.

I sighed and then gave in to the laughter that bubbled up. The sound of it carried an edge of madness. "Yes, actually. My mate bond has been very troublesome since it activated."

It was his turn to be stunned, and he blinked at me several times before laughing so hard he scattered a bunch of animals and had to wipe tears from the comers of his eyes. "Well good. I'm glad you're a quicker study than I was, at least. Poor Rylan was in such denial he had to do a spell before he believed it."

I huffed a breath, simultaneously relieved and terrified at having admitted it out loud to someone else. "She's human. Gifted. Special."

"And?"

"I'm ... we are not the same."

"Perhaps, but I'd wager you're also not that different. Or, if you are, there is good balance there. Have some faith in the Fates, my son. They rarely make mistakes."

"Not never?"

He shook his head, ancient wisdom and sadness in his eyes. "Nothing is infallible, Coltor. You know that as well as I do."

I rolled my shoulders, trying to chase some of the tension away. "We hardly know one another."

He shrugged. "So, get familiar. It's not as hard as you're making it."

"She's ..." I trailed off, unable to get the words out, but my glance at the door betrayed me.

His large hand patted my shoulder again. "She'll be alright. Nobody in this family knows how to fail when it comes to taking care of our own."

I nodded, and after another moment of staring directly into my soul, he departed, leaving me an exhausted mess on my own porch.

THE NEXT COUPLE of days brought a constant stream of company. It should have made me uncomfortable, but it was strangely nice to not be the only one in charge of thinking through logistics.

Platters and baskets arrived courtesy of Grace, holding meals and snacks enough to tide the entire population of the glade over for several days. It took all three of our kitchens to store it all, and there was never a time when I felt even slightly more than peckish before I had tea and something to eat in my hand.

After some deliberation with Hailon, I'd taken Merry back to her own cabin. There was more space, and it was closer both to the portal and their cabin. Besides that, it was easier for Hailon to help her friend with things like bathing in the larger bathroom. We were feeding her broth, spoonfuls at a time, while helping her swallow. It gave us both a purpose, doing those things that were still necessary, despite how fully her body seemed to have shut down.

Progress was infinitesimal, but she did start opening her eyes a little bit more starting on the second day. I could tell by her breathing when she was asleep and when she was awake, but other than that, there was no indication of change. I took her outside, so she could see that her plants were cared for. Hailon or I did the watering, but it seemed the animals had taken the job of weeding and insect control on themselves. I narrated my every action when I was the one with her, speaking more during those hours than I had in several years combined. I wanted nothing more than for her to say something back.

The third day, Greta visited with her raven, Belmont. He and the birds hanging about on Merry's roof had quite a rousing conversation, and then he perched on the porch railing like a king addressing his subjects.

Greta, who was organizing several vials of elixir on Merry's kitchen table, looked at him curiously. The door was open, and the chatter of the animals camped in her yard was a steady background noise. The pile of gifts had migrated to her porch, an ever-growing mound of berries, flowers, stones and a multitude of shiny objects. I appreciated the gesture but still wanted them all gone.

"Belmont?" she inquired, seeing him open his wings wide and stalk from one side to the other as he made that peculiar corvid knocking sound. Greta stilled, eyes a bit glassy as she communicated with her bird. "Oh," she breathed finally, and one of the falcons swooped down and dropped something on the steps. She picked up the item, holding it up for me to see.

The band was broken, one whole strand of the braid undone, but I recognized it immediately. "Merry's bracelet? Where did they find that?"

"Was it missing?" she asked.

"Yes. I don't know how long, but I noticed it was gone after she collapsed."

"It's leaking magic," she said frowning. "I don't know how else to describe it. Not necessarily anything bad, it feels protective in a way, but it's ... odd. May I have Rylan examine it?"

"Of course." Greta grimaced and pocketed the jewelry while Belmont did another display. The animals quieted, several small groups wandering further away. "Is something happening?"

"I don't understand completely, but they're telling Belmont that Merry is ... keeping something? There's something about a celebration. No, a ceremony."

"Keeper?" I frowned.

"Maybe?" She squinted, listening. "Yes, that's it. Keeper."

"There's not been one for eons. Are you sure?"

Greta shrugged. "That's what he says. Belmont?" The bird tilted his head, using his one good eye to take in his mistress. "You and Archimedes weren't drawn to come here, not like them. Why?" The knocking changed to trilling, then he went quiet. "I see." She frowned, sagging a bit. "We should have been asking them more questions. I'm so sorry."

"What did he say?"

"They were not drawn because they're already bonded, but they would have been compelled to attend the ceremony out of respect." Her eyes strayed to Merry and stayed there. "We failed her. All of us. She came to us, with that book. We knew she was starting to hear them speak to her, I should have thought to ask—"

"She was regularly seeing Ophelia, living with her even, at first. There was no reason for you to interrogate your bird."

"The moment she mentioned animals it should have occurred to one of us to check with them. So foolish." She turned, hand trembling as she pointed at the vials and very efficiently instructed me on their use. "I'm sorry, Coltor. I promise we'll do everything we can for her."

I knew she meant it. I gave her a grateful nod, and she leaned in for a quick hug before she made her escape, the tension in her spine familiar as she strode away. Belmont took flight to chase after her. She was kin, after all, and I could recognize that particular brand of self-loathing-fueled anger anywhere. It was the kind that got things done. My sisters both looked much the same when similarly motivated.

Father was right, this family didn't fail, and I was rapidly remembering that our circle included far more than the stone kin I was used to labeling with that word. A null, an earth witch, a human, and several demons had also joined the clan. Some very officially, in fact. Euphemia had put my father and Grace, Vassago and Greta, and Rylan and Calla all through the kin welcoming ceremony not so long ago.

I smiled and allowed hope to grow roots.

BY THE FOURTH night, I'd become unbearably restless.

Nothing had changed, and I was tired of just sitting around. I'd spent one whole evening trying and failing to produce a vision intentionally. I'd screamed my demands to the sky, insistent that I was owed a glimpse of what might happen from here. The Fates denied each and every request.

I had one last idea for something that might help her, not to mention several things I wanted to say tearing at my chest to get out. After everyone had gone their own way for the night, and my father was running my patrol, I scooped Merry and her blanket up in my arms and took her to the heart of the old castle, where the sparkling magic felt strongest.

I sat cross-legged with Merry in my lap, right where all the doorways were hidden in the fallen stones. As the warm, pleasant prickle of magic washed over us, I closed my eyes and just breathed with her, the slow pulse of her heartbeat matching mine.

After several minutes, her eyes opened, the deep brown orbs still gazing into the distance instead of at me, but it was something.

"This is King Emankor's great hall." I smirked, the notion amusing, considering it looked like nothing more than a few half-buried floor stones and rubble. "I like it here. Very much." Merry's rhythmic blinks gave away nothing, but I knew she was listening. I needed her to still be herself, and like the mundane narration of our daily activities, this felt like it might help. "Belmont said something about you being Keeper, which is something I honestly believed to be long gone. Explains the animals, though." I sighed. "I hate that everything happening to you right now is out of your control. Or mine. It's all driven by the Fates, which seems terribly unfair. What if you don't even want it?" I focused on the buzz of power along my skin, the chill of the stone underneath me. "Everything is so strange, Merry. Ophelia is still stone sleeping, and you're not well." I breathed in deeply, her scent and the tang of the magic filling my lungs as I donned my bravery. "I need you to come back to me, Firebird. It's not right here without you. *I'm* not right without you."

My father's silhouette crossed above us, his wings out wide as he checked the boundaries of the ruins. A long breath leaked out of me, and I sagged, tightening my arms around her body, pulling her into me. Her head rested against my shoulder, her eyes on the sky.

"I'm a coward, Merry." I closed my eyes, forehead against hers. "I should have told you things, but I didn't know how. Not even when

I was given a perfect opportunity. That day, when you touched my hand at d'Arcan, I had a vision. That's why I visit Ophelia. She's been helping me navigate this terrible new gift. I'm pretty hopeless so far at figuring it out. In that vision ..." I swallowed. "I found you by the pools. You were dead." I choked on my words. "That's why I was so scared that day when you were only sleeping. I thought my worst fear had come true.

"But you were okay, and I got too comfortable. I decided maybe I'd just seen a different possible outcome, because I had a vision of Ophelia dead too, and she's only stone sleeping." I paused, realizing that Merry's condition was not terribly different than stone sleep.

"There's something more, and I shouldn't tell you all this when you can't respond to me, but like I said, I'm a coward. You're special, Merry. A gift in your own right. I don't know if your people have anything similar in their customs, but you are my mate. I can feel it in my bones." I spread her hand flat over my heart and covered it with mine. "This is where the bond lives. And I ..." Words failed, because what else could I say that would adequately explain such a thing? "Between the two things, plus everything else going on in the glade, I was scared. I still am, if I'm being honest, probably always will be. I know who you're meant to be to me, what I can be to you, if you choose." The stars twinkled above us, a cool breeze moving her curls. "The choice *is* yours. If you don't want this, I will understand, and that will be the end of it." My heart cracked at the thought, but I meant every word.

"If you need some time, I would not begrudge you that either, of course. What you need, what you want, matters most, and too much has been required of you without your consent." I leaned forward and kissed her forehead, the bond flaring hot. "It's unfair to tell you all this now. I know that. But you needed to know. And no matter what your choice is, I will do anything I can to bring you back to yourself."

Lighter for having said what I needed to, I shifted us around, using one of the old pillars as a backrest, and settled in. The breeze had kicked up, so I let my wings out, wrapping us up inside them. I didn't want Merry to be cold.

Power continued to sparkle around us, the faint pulse of the ancient dwelling's magic a steady beat through my body. I hoped it was doing the same in hers, that somehow, this magic would cure her. I nodded off, or I thought I had, when a vision burst through me, leaving fire in my veins.

She would be fine. She had to be. The Fates had gifted me a look into a future that was too beautiful to exist without her in it.

"COLTOR?" THE SWEETEST voice invaded my restless dreams, pulling me back to awareness.

Faint traces of orange predawn streaked the sky. Merry was still tucked into her blanket in my lap, my wings a protective shield around us both. But unlike the past several days, she was looking *at* me.

My heart stuttered, and without any hesitation, I cupped her face in my palm. "Merry?"

"Hi."

Joy bounced through me, I squeezed her tighter to my chest, dotting the side of her face with featherlight kisses. "There you are. I've been so worried. We all have." She grimaced through a tight smile, and I tensed. "What do you need?"

"Head hurts. Thirsty." It seemed to take a lot from her to speak, her voice rusty and slow.

"Of course." Urgency crashed through me as I scrambled to my feet, holding her body as close to mine as I could as I lifted us off the ground with my wings, gliding us back to her cabin.

Once inside, I settled her in a dining chair instead of the sofa at her insistence, though it was against my better judgment. I hastily gathered water, tea, a selection of Grace's food, and broth, putting it all on the table in front of her. Her coordination was still very poor, so I pulled my chair right up beside hers and helped steady her hand when it trembled under the weight of the glass. Her brown eyes held my face as I guided the water to her mouth.

"Don't like this, either," she managed after several careful sips, tears in her eyes.

"I'm sure it hurts your pride, I know it would mine, but you're doing fantastically. Just a few hours ago you couldn't even open your eyes when you wanted to." I fed her a small bite of honey cake with my fingers, trying to ignore the flash of heat that passed through me as her lips grazed my skin. "Tell me what you need. I'll get it for you. Anything."

"Medicine?"

I nearly broke the chair I got up so quickly to fetch the elixir. Once she'd had a good dose, she started to slump.

"Tired?"

She nodded, eyes slowly closing.

"Let's get you in bed then."

Stubborn indeed, she insisted on walking instead of having me carry her. She hugged the wall and shuffled into the bathroom first.

Her words were soft as I pulled up the blanket on her bed. "Thank you."

She was out before her next breath, and I exhaled what felt like the first full breath since I'd found her by the pools.

CHAPTER 17
MERRY

FOR SOMEONE WHO had done almost nothing but sleep for the better part of a week, I was unreasonably exhausted. Healing was best done while resting, sure, but I was tired of being tired. I woke again sometime near midday and forced myself to get up before I slipped back to sleep. After a very slow, deliberate walk to the bathroom, re-learning how to make my body move how I wanted it to, I returned to the main room and found Coltor napping on my sofa. I approached him slowly, trying to keep from disturbing him. I wanted a moment to examine the man who'd cared for me with such gentle dedication. It was only by luck when I bumped one of the dining chairs, he remained unbothered.

His sharply angled features were softened by sleep, but not by much. One of his legs had slipped off the cushions, and his booted foot was flat on the floor, the opposite arm flung up over his head. It was adorable but made me feel bad that someone of his size had to make do with such improperly fitted furniture when he was surely exhausted. The poor man hadn't left my side except for short times since my mind had splintered.

I turned and went to fetch myself some of the elixir and more water, cheeks hot with a blush. His tender care had almost certainly helped put me back together, and there was no ignoring how that made me feel.

As I was staring some more, debating whether or not I felt well enough to eat something or perhaps go check my plants, there was a mighty scuffle outside. The heavy beat of hooves against the ground and a distant but familiar whinny had me tripping toward the door.

Coltor woke with a start, on his feet nearly the moment he opened his eyes. "Merry?"

"I'm fine," I said, my voice still full of gravel and slow to work.

He followed my movements toward the door with his eyes, confusion rapidly changing to concern. "Are you sure you're ready for that?"

"You took me."

"I did. But I warned them to keep to themselves first."

"They didn't hurt me. Not on purpose." I twitched a grin at his indignant glare. "Jacks." My horse's whinny carried through the open window again.

Coltor moved quickly enough he was out the door before me, an arm around my waist for support as I shuffled onto the porch. My limbs worked but still felt as though they were weighed down by stones.

My horse was misbehaving mightily as he plowed down the path, stomping and causing a terrible scene. Most concerning, it appeared he had a rider while being so erratic.

"Jacks!" I tried to yell, but my damaged throat didn't allow for much volume.

"*Ophelia?*" Coltor breathed the sorceress's name with incredulity, making sure my hands were both gripping the porch railing before leaving me to greet the visitors.

The animals had mostly fled from the ruckus, but those remaining were clearly curious about the horse's presence. Jacks was clearly upset, breaths coming in snorts, and the skin on his back jumping in agitation.

Coltor helped Ophelia dismount, and Jacks settled enough to walk over to where I was standing. He stared at me for a moment, then lowered his nose. Emotion welled up as I pressed my forehead to his.

Never frighten me like that again, mistress. The voice rang rich and clear in my head, full of authority and power. *I should have come with you straightaway, no matter my disdain for those terrible portals. And I should have gotten rid of that wrist bangle of yours ages ago, brought you somewhere they could help with your gift long before now.*

"Jacks?" I gasped, pulling away. He backed up half a step, meeting my eye with one of his, the intelligence there familiar but also shockingly new. "Saints." I breathed in and out several times, a wave of dizziness passing through me. "Did you always do that?"

I speak to you often, mistress. You always seemed to understand me fine, even if you didn't hear me in this way. I am glad you can now, though. Are you alright? Does this hurt you?

"I'm okay." Tears sprang to my eyes, and I rested my forehead against his again for a moment.

I tried to tell you what they wanted, what you are. I'm sorry.

"Oh, Jacks."

There will be a ceremony soon. To welcome you properly as Keeper. That's what they're all gathering for and waiting on. They all want to officially pledge their loyalty to you. It is a high honor.

Hearing the truth of the matter straight out was a bit jarring, but it was a relief to finally know what was going on. Jacks snorted at my silence.

You can refuse, mistress. It is a big ask. They should not have overwhelmed you. There just hasn't been one in so long, they were careless in their enthusiasm.

"What exactly does a Keeper do?"

Jacks shifted his weight, wise eyes blinking slowly. Several of the closest animals perked up, and I could hear murmurs of their thoughts. They were still apologetic, full of kind greetings. *In simplest terms, they keep the balance. Between species, between the creatures and the earth. It's like maintaining a very large, extended family in many ways. Occasionally there's a very big decision to be made, important details to sort out. Mostly it's just allowing them to lead their lives, build their families, as long as it's happening in a way that respects the world around them. There are the familiar bonds as well, of course.* He clearly saw my hesitation. *I will be there with you, mistress. As will your friends. The stone kin. You will not be expected to do any of it alone.*

Heartened, I found myself nodding. I'd never done anything significant before, and this felt simultaneously far too big for me and like it was exactly what I'd been preparing for.

"I'm honored to be chosen."

I am proud to know you, mistress. I believe you will excel as Keeper. He made that noise that was oddly like laughter again, then glanced around, judgment heavy in the way he peered at the other creatures. *I have some things to discuss with them. They should not have frightened you. They should have spoken to anyone willing to listen so as not to overwhelm you. It will not happen again.*

"Oh. Thank you, Jacks."

He turned and ambled off, head swinging back and forth. The animals in his path seemed to snap to attention, gathering around him as he moved away from my yard and down the path toward the meadow and pools.

"Jacks?" He paused, head turned my way. "Are you my ... familiar?"

He tossed his head a few times, making a sound that was suspiciously like a laugh.

You are my chosen bonded, mistress. Perhaps you can speak to the demon and have him make us an official contract? Descendants of The Stallion get special permissions.

I choked on a laugh in surprise. "Alright." I blinked. "Can we please come back to your lineage at some point? I'd like to discuss that."

He seemed amused. *Of course.* Jacks bobbed his head Coltor's direction. *I like him. I trust him. He will care for you appropriately.* He moved on along down the path, full entourage of animals going with him.

I could only stare after him, too stunned to do anything else.

"Well. Seems we're on our way then," Ophelia said, sounding pleased. "That beast was mightily upset about me taking such a long nap. Poked his head in my windows all times of day to be sure I was still there."

"We were all very worried about you," Coltor said.

"*Tsk.* An old woman should be able to rest if she likes."

"You were locked in stone sleep for *weeks*. That's cause for concern," he countered.

"So all my wonderful kin have told me, every time they came to visit and make sure I hadn't yet returned to the stones. Lovely to be so worried over, honestly. Even if it was unwarranted."

"Why not come out of your rest to reassure someone, then?" Coltor's tone was downright sassy, and I watched the flash of horror cross his face with amusement.

Ophelia laughed. "Because I don't owe anyone an explanation for anything I do." And what could even be said about that really? Coltor's mouth slammed shut, his jaw clenched. She glanced between us. "Have you figured it out then?" Ophelia asked, the question aimed at Coltor specifically, a lopsided smile on her mouth.

"I have." He sighed. "Well, the mate part. My gift is still mostly a mystery to me."

She laughed, reaching up to pat his cheek. "That will come, nephew. In due time." Ophelia turned to me. "And your recovery?"

"As good as can be expected," I said with a shrug, glad she hadn't asked me about the mate bond. I'd heard every word that night, but we hadn't had a chance to speak of it any further. "Tea?"

She nodded, allowing Coltor to take her by the hand as she climbed my porch steps. "Indeed." I hoped Coltor had some whiskey at his hut he could run to get for her, otherwise she'd be very disappointed in my brew.

Coltor's wide eyes met mine as he led her through the door. Without a word being shared, I understood his expression.

The sorceress had left her heavily warded home for the first time in memory. My horse, a descendant of a mythical being, whom I could now hear speaking to me in my head, had used a portal to bring her here. I was the first Keeper in an age. What fresh hell were we in for next?

BY THE TIME Coltor returned with a bottle of whiskey from his stash, I had brewed three pots of tea, and the cabin was close to bursting it was so full.

Hailon and Seir had arrived as quickly as they could after seeing Jacks trotting through the glade. Seir had propped a small mirror up on the low sofa table, and inside the glass were the residents of d'Arcan minus Magnus, who had shown up shortly after Hailon and Seir. Coltor's sisters, Imogen and Lovette, had knocked on my door not long after him. All we were missing was Tap. There was truly no space at all for more company should any arrive—we'd be serving tea out of bowls and off plates to guests seated on my bed if they did.

Everyone had insisted I sit, so Ophelia, Hailon, and I were cozied up on the little sofa with Magnus and Coltor standing at our backs. Seir was sitting on the floor so he could see into the mirror, and Imogen and Lovette were at my little dining table.

"Your bracelet," Rylan said through the glass, "acted as a protective charm. The stone itself—"

"What kind of stone?" Imogen asked, leaning so she could see the mirror.

"Red jasper," I supplied. She nodded as though this in itself was an explanation, then settled back into her seat. Imogen and

I had shared only a brief greeting, but she seemed very kind. She strongly resembled both Coltor and Magnus.

"Yes, that stone has protective properties, but there was also magic woven in. The hair in the band." He tilted his head. "Where did it come from?"

"Everyone," I said, my voice improved by the tea, which Ophelia had splashed with whiskey for me after Coltor handed over the bottle to her and turned his back. "I don't know exactly how far back, but there were strands from most of my father's family line, his included, and mine. There's even some from Jacks. The bracelet always passed to the eldest child."

He nodded in understanding. "The inclusion of each owner's hair likely provided its own kind of magic, but I'm guessing part of the inheritance tradition included a blessing. Even with some distance from the original witch in the line, or perhaps with new additions along the way, that many contributors layering a spell made it quite powerful."

As I processed that, Ophelia perked up beside me. "Powerful enough to make it so she can't feel my wards?"

Rylan nodded thoughtfully. "Hard to say without knowing exactly what incantation was used, but it's possible." Ophelia grumbled.

"Is that why I could read the book after I lost it? Why I heard all the animals so loudly? They truly didn't mean to hurt me." I was likely repeating myself on that point, but it felt necessary. "It was just that everything was magnified and I couldn't tolerate it."

"Yes, that's likely. Removing that protective charm, and whatever spells were embedded in it, allowed you to feel the full force of your gift. The muffled, slow trickle became a flood."

Ophelia frowned. "All this trouble because nobody could read the blasted book?" When that was confirmed, she huffed irritably, then turned to me all sugar sweet and patted my hand. "Apologies, Merry. I didn't know only conduits could read it."

"It's not your fault." I was reminded of her comment from that day in her hut, that my magic would need training and support. I'd done nothing to train, and the bracelet blocking much out was not as helpful as actual support.

"Any idea what changed that allowed Merry to awaken?" Vassago asked.

"She was certainly fighting on her own already, but I took her to the heart," Coltor said quietly.

"The heart?" Rylan queried.

"Castle Emankor," I supplied, realizing that the warm wash of bubbly tingles I'd felt while held in his arms under the stars that night had been from more than his confessions and affection.

"The magic there is quite potent. I didn't know whether or not it would do anything to help, but I had to try."

Ophelia startled everyone by clapping her hands together loudly. "Well done, lad."

"Perhaps regular visits are a good idea?" Rylan suggested.

"Yes, yes. That would certainly be good to help you recover after using your ability, Merry. Especially until you learn to manage it." Ophelia nodded enthusiastically, barely avoiding spilling some of her freshly-poured tea.

"I will take her as often as she wants," Coltor promised, his hand coming to rest warmly on my shoulder.

There was a bit more conversation around me, explanations of magic and warding and things my tired mind was too mushy to grasp. I focused on the table before me, trying to digest all of the things I'd learned in such a short time. Before I realized, the place had emptied out.

Coltor squatted in front of me, concern etched in his sharp features. "You okay?"

I nodded. "I think so. Just tired."

"I was going to go out for a bit with Ophelia, work on the wards. But it can wait." He reached out and took one of my hands into his.

"No, you go. I'll be fine. I'm going to take a nap."

"You could rest in the heart while we work. Take in more magic."

I smiled at him, the earnest expression in his wide eyes. "No, that's alright. I'd rather use the comfortable bed here if you'll be busy doing other things." Coltor's mouth dropped open, his cheeks grew pink and he huffed a breath.

"If you're sure." His brows drew together. "But maybe you should—"

"I'm really fine, I promise. Just tired." I chuckled. "When did you start being this worried about me?"

"Since I met you." The answer was immediate, the look in his eyes sincere.

"Oh." My whole body flared with heat. For all my surety about not needing a man, that I could do it all by myself ... his version of partnership sure was tempting. I inhaled, pulling up my bravery to broach a topic that had been quietly itching at the back of my thoughts. "Can we talk later?"

His eyes turned sad, and he let go of my hand, like he was bracing for something devastating. "Of course."

"It's nothing bad. Just about some of the things you told me out there." He swallowed, and I could see fear in his dark eyes. I didn't want him to leave so upset, so I blurted, "Coltor, do you want to be my mate?"

"Yes."

"That simple? No hesitation?"

"Nothing in my life has ever been simpler, even when it's quite possibly the most unexpected, messy, beautiful thing I've ever been faced with."

I couldn't help but smile.

He warred with himself for a moment, then surprised me by grabbing my face with both hands and kissing me. His lips were firm at first, like he was worried I'd pull away. I covered one of his hands with mine and leaned in, encouraging him with small swipes of my tongue, a tilt of my head. It didn't take much before we were tasting one another's breath and mapping each other's mouths with teeth and tongues.

Coltor pulled away on a groan and got to his feet. "If I don't go now, I won't at all, but we will talk about this as much as you want later."

"Alright. It's definitely wise not to keep Ophelia waiting. I hear she's pretty dangerous."

"You are too, Firebird," he said, ducking down for one final kiss.

Then he was out the door, leaving me steeped in his scent and feeling more alive than I'd felt in a very long time.

CHAPTER 18
COLTOR

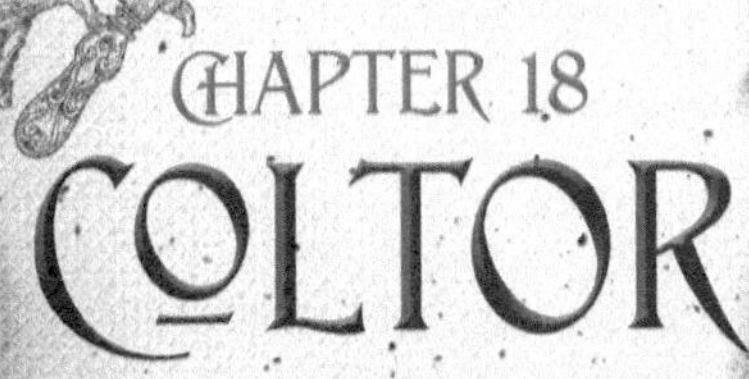

"WHY IS SHE here?" Ophelia complained, crossing her arms as another gargoyle, one that looked quite a lot like her, crossed the glade.

"Euphemia is the mistress of ceremonies," Lovette said, clucking her tongue. "You know that as well as I do."

Ophelia tsked and tried to turn away, but Lovette and Imogen flanked her. "It's only for the ceremony," Imogen said calmly.

My sisters were bolder than anyone else dared to be with our elder, and she tolerated it from them for some reason the rest of us weren't aware of.

"Hello, Ophelia," the woman greeted her from a safe distance. "Yes, hello."

"Be nice!" Lovette hissed under her breath. "Bury this thing festering between you once and for all, it's not healthy to hang onto such ugliness."

My father and I both tensed, worried that this might be the thing that sent the ancient into a rage. After a long moment, where it seemed nobody breathed—the demons on the fringes of our group included—Ophelia shook my sisters off and approached hers.

"Which version of the speech are you planning?" Ophelia asked.

"The modified of course. Nobody wants to sit through the original. Too stodgy and dated." Euphemia curled her lip as though the thought disgusted her.

"Good."

They stood there staring at one another, stone kin hundreds of years old looking very much like children too stubborn to apologize over breaking the other's toy.

"Would you like to help me prepare?"

"If you like. I can perhaps give some valuable input."

"Of course you can. You always could, Ophelia."

Ophelia stared at her sister, mouth set in a tight line. "That's not—"

"I know what I said all those years ago, but that's not what I meant. Not then, not now, not ever."

Ophelia squinted, debating. Then she stepped forward, chin lifted. "Fine. I'll help."

Leaving the rest of us to finally breathe, the pair moved off toward the pools to continue their conversation.

"Mind the path," I warned several of my kin walking through. Some carried big planks to be used for tables and benches, others toted metal rods for cooking spits and barrels of wine and ale.

To hold a ceremony was to celebrate, and to celebrate required copious amounts of food and drink. My kin were nothing if not consistent for their love of those things in equal measure. And when stone kin were motivated to celebrate, they could accomplish just about anything, very, very quickly.

Since Merry's mind was too fragile for her to use the portal and all the animals were here anyway, my kin were bringing all the tools needed for celebrating from the conclave to the glade. It had barely been a day, and preparations were nearly complete.

The glade had been flooded with people coming and going once again. Every available dwelling was open to be used for rest, food, planning. My hut was the only exception, it was deemed too far from the activity, much to my relief. The new cabins had been outfitted with furniture and staples by the aunts, simply out of necessity for them to be functional. The matriarchs were spread through the kitchens, providing expert direction on just about everything. I'd seen Grace and Jorna paired up at one point, both pointing agitated fingers and scowling as they barked orders to terrified men half their age and twice their size. I was amused but also thankful I was not one of them.

"I need a drink," my father breathed, right before stalking off toward Rylan and Vassago, who were watching with the same tense interest as the rest of us. Well, except for my sisters; they were smiling as though thoroughly pleased.

"Is Merry prepared?" Lovette asked.

"She says she is."

"You don't agree?" Imogen asked, fingers tapping along the leather of her vest.

"I think she needs more time to heal. All of this has happened very quickly, and she's barely on her feet again."

"It will be more peaceful once the ceremony is done." Lovette patted my shoulder as she walked past me. "We'll go check on her."

"I have a gift for her anyhow," Imogen said with a grin.

I turned a stern look on my sister, knowing full well she had a blade hidden somewhere on her person for Merry. "What kind?"

She chuffed. "The perfect for her kind."

"Big or small, Imo? I'm already on my last frayed nerve here."

My sisters laughed at me outright. "We know," Lovette said. "You were already experiencing some terrible symptoms when we saw you last."

"Symptoms?" I balked.

"It was written all over you," Imo confirmed with a nod. "The irrational agitation, the grumpiness."

"The chest rubbing, the denial." Lovette flourished a hand.

"Very obvious you were falling for her. Emotions and mate bonds are tricky like that sometimes. Trust me, I know."

I scowled at them both. "I'm not grumpy."

They glanced at one another and fell into raucous laughter. Imogen basically keeping Lovette from falling to the ground at one point. "If you say so, little brother." Imogen produced a small blade similar to Hailon's herb knife from a sheath on her belt. It would be put to good use in Merry's hands while she gardened, as well as for protection. It was a perfect little belt knife. I swore, promising to do my best not to worry over it.

"You work fast." I turned it over in my hands, her impeccable craftsmanship impressive as always. Where the leather-wrapped handle met the blade at the bolster was a piece of red jasper.

"I had the steel mostly done already, just waiting for the right purpose. Rylan agreed to give me the stone when he was done with his examination of her bracelet." Her gentle smile expressed how proud she was of her work.

"What happened to the rest of it?" I asked, knowing Merry had been very attached to the jewelry, but it had been beyond repairing to its original state.

"Brom needed more time, but he's incorporating what he can into a sheath for her."

"That's very kind of him. Is he here?"

My older sister blushed as she took the blade back from me. "No, he's at the outpost finishing commissions for the armory."

I needed to make time to visit with the leathersmith, it would seem. I'd like to get to know the man who'd managed to capture Imo's affection.

"One would think such a celebration would allow a day off, but no." Lovette frowned. At least my sisters had one another to complain about the demands of the outpost with. "Come on." Lovette tugged on Imogen's sleeve, and they went off toward Merry's cabin.

I took a deep breath and waded into the fray, joining my father and the demons under Grace's watchful eye and stern direction.

"SHE'S FINE." LOVETTE patted my hand as Merry was escorted up onto the little platform and seated between Ophelia and Jorna. "She insisted she was ready, we checked with her several times. She's smiling even."

"She smiled through terrible headaches for who knows how long," I countered, still upset with myself for not noticing what she was going through sooner.

"Fine, but she's literally sitting with Ophelia. And her horse is just there." Lovette pointed off to the side of the platform, where Jacks stood, bedecked in a floral garland woven from all the wildflowers that grew in the glade, looking very regal. Both Belmont and Archimedes were perched in a small tree on the other side, and Morticia was lounging near Jacks's hooves. "And all the creatures are orderly and behaving themselves."

It was my father who spoke up next. "Rylan gave her a spelled trinket to hold if she feels overwhelmed—it will filter some of the voices out, protect her mind." That brought some relief.

"Her new blade has the jasper in it too," Imogen added.

"We're all here, watching." I turned at Hailon's voice, and found that all the demons, including Tap, had arrived and were settling in near us, as were their equally powerful wives. "Nothing is going to happen to her. And if she seems at all distressed, we'll stop everything. Take her away from the ceremony." She squeezed my arm, and the flurry of bees in my chest quieted.

"Nobody wants to see her hurt, Coltor," Greta added, sadness still etched into her face. I hated that she blamed herself for not checking in with the familiars.

"Who's minding the doorways?" I asked Seir, while looking at Tap.

The crossroads demon fidgeted, looking as uncomfortable away from his station as I often felt. And that wasn't even considering he was one of four demons in a very large gathering of stone kin. We'd become quite cordial for beings that were once sworn enemies.

"I called in a favor with my unit leader—they're doing what they can from Hell. The rest will wait a few hours." He glanced at his brother and whispered, "He needs to blow off some steam."

"It's a miracle you got him to leave," Vassago teased.

Tap's nose wrinkled. "I attended Rylan's wedding not all that long ago. Left me with a mighty mess, but I did it."

"I'll help you with any resulting problems," Seir reassured him.

Tap nodded and settled between Seir and Rylan. "You absolutely will."

Several stone kin had turned to look at the gathering of demons. They were not strangers to the conclave, and were officially kin, but for many of our kind, we were still getting used to being among them as friends.

The sun was setting, tossing the glade into glorious shades of orange and red, bathing Merry in the light that suited her beauty the best. Euphemia commanded everyone's attention from atop a wide tree stump that had been placed for later use as a table.

"It is known that throughout the ages, those of us with magic have been friends with the creatures of the earth. Much of that time, there was a Keeper, a special witch or stone kin—sometimes both at once—that was master or mistress of all the beasts. They were the ones to address quarrels and help ensure that the balance is kept." Euphemia tipped her head to the side. "As much as one can anyhow. Nature does much of that herself, after all.

"In the beginning, there was Helgarth, who accidentally bonded himself to a bear and became the first beast master of the stone kin. After him came Morghan, a witch, who cared for all creatures from a bog in the far south, near the gates." Euphemia sped through several more generations, moving on when Ophelia tugged on her sleeve, giving a look that embodied the annoyance of an older sister. When I snorted, Imogen turned and stared, eyebrow raised, the same tone conveyed perfectly.

"We've gone without such an incredible soul for a great many years, but the Fates have seen fit to bring us Merry. Let us all welcome her!" There was a cheer, and even the animals participated. "Merry, do you understand what is being asked of you?"

"Yes, I do."

"Will you care for the creatures to the best of your ability? Address bond requests and manage disputes?"

"I will."

"And you, creatures of the earth, do you accept Merry as your Keeper, and do you promise to respond to her call if necessary? To treat her with care, and kindness so she can be with you as long as possible?" The noise was immense as the animals responded. "Wonderful. May the greetings and celebration begin!"

There was another cheer, and Ophelia steered Merry to a seat in the shade. Jacks came over and stood at her side, Calla's cat sitting near her feet. Greta and Rylan's birds remained in the tree, watching over it all.

"Pardon me," Tap said, excusing himself and striding over to Merry's side. He bowed to Ophelia, movements graceful and well-practiced. He said something to Merry that made her eyes go round, but she nodded enthusiastically and accepted a letter he pulled from his pocket.

"It's a promotion," Seir said with a broad smile. "He's offering her the authority to approve the bonds on his behalf."

"Can he do that?"

"Of course he can," Vassago answered. "He always could, he just never trusted anyone enough to let go of control before." His mouth curled into a smile. "He's still the final say, mind, but there won't be a reason for him to intervene or seal them individually unless there's an issue."

"It will be good for him." Rylan's smile was serene. "He was doing far too many things."

Tap turned to the animals, explaining what was happening without opening his mouth. There was a gentle ripple through them, as though they'd given their permission for the transfer of power. He bowed again and stepped back, standing behind her chair but still present.

The animals approached Merry in families or pairs, each performing what stood for their kind as a polite nod or bow. Many brought another gift, like the ones they'd left on her porch. She smiled each and every time, looking them all in the eyes as she spoke to them. Despite her positive expression, worry set it's claws in deep that she was going to wear out long before she'd gotten through all the creatures.

The audience began to break down and move toward the tables of food and drink. Chatter grew and focus dwindled as the celebration began for everyone except the person it was for.

She smiled at me as I approached, the animals allowing me plenty of space. "Do you need anything?"

"I'm okay." She met my eye. "I'm fine, I promise."

I glanced at my elder and the demon, and they both just gave a tilt of their heads. I saw it then, the way both Ophelia and Tap had a hand on Merry. I nodded back, understanding. They were channeling what strength they could to her, balancing the effect the creatures had on her with their own abilities.

Satisfied, at least for the moment, I went to fill her a plate.

IT TOOK SEVERAL hours for Merry to meet all the creatures, but she'd done it without incident and with grace. Most departed not long after performing the rite, which left me both relieved and worried about what all she might have agreed to during that time. Tap had scribbled some notes as well, so I was certain she had quite a job ahead of her.

I'd swept her off to eat and drink as soon as possible, relieved to have her back in my care. She was quiet and watchful but felt like herself.

The party proceeded enthusiastically the whole time, my kin laughing and dancing, eating and drinking. The noise was starting to wear on my nerves, but I did enjoy seeing everyone have such a good time.

It was growing late, but I knew things would continue until at least the wee hours if not straight through to the next day when cleanup started.

Ophelia and Euphemia were cloistered away at a little table by themselves, catching up on several decades' worth of gossip. The demons had strong-armed Tap into sitting down to eat, but he'd refused to stay longer than it took him to finish his food and a single drink. The d'Arcan residents had departed not long after he returned to the crossroads, though Seir was clearly in his element and thankfully could stumble home whenever he chose.

Merry and I ended up on the ground up against some of the stones near the pools, close enough to feel like we were part of the goings-on but far enough that we weren't in the middle of things.

The longer the night stretched on, the more she started to sag into herself, tightness at the edges of her eyes.

"You don't have to stay, you know. Stone kin are known to continue celebrating through the night and into the next day." I watched the panic take hold, her eyes wide and breathing quicker.

"That long?."

"Come on." I stood and reached out a hand, pulling her to her feet.

Several people bowed or clapped as we passed through, but nobody asked us to stay. The further we got from the revelry, the stiffer her steps became.

"Merry?" I couldn't help the worry that laced my tone.

"I'm just tired."

I let my wings out and opened my arms. Despite the flare of discomfort from the bond, I couldn't help the wave of pride and pleasure that washed over me when she came straight into my embrace and threw her arms around my neck.

"Take me home, please?" Nothing had ever sounded sweeter or made my blood pound as hard in my throat as those words.

I scooped her up against me and pumped my wings, chasing up plumes of dust. "As you wish, Firebird. Whatever you need."

CHAPTER 19
MERRY

OPHELIA HAD WARNED me, as had Tap, but being told was completely different than seeing it for myself. I leaned into the mirror, heart pounding as I examined the area under my collarbone. Symbols had appeared on my skin, painless ink the color of flames. They were simple but beautiful, all organic swirls and dots.

As I traced over them with my fingers, the bathroom door burst open. "Merry? Are you—" Coltor stopped in the doorway, clearly horrified with himself for repeating something that had caused tension between us, debating what the correct next action should be. "You shouted."

"It's fine." I was wrapped in a towel, my hair wet down my back. I chuckled at how we'd ended up back here again, just under very different circumstances. "You can come in."

Cautiously, he stepped forward. His eyes widened and he approached me slowly, his gaze trained on the mirror.

He stretched out a finger toward my skin but stopped before touching. "They're lovely. And they're the same color as your hair, Firebird."

"Is that why you call me that? My hair?"

"In part." Coltor rocked back on his heels, crossing his arms as though trying to keep himself from reaching out again. "It's your hair, certainly, but also the way the sun often lights you up in such a way that you remind me of that creature. You hold your arms like wings, and a trick of the light gives you blazing feathers ..." He trailed off, features pinching like he'd said more than he intended. "This mark." Rough fingertips traced along the birthmark on my back. "It looks like a feather." His eyes lingered on the curve of my shoulders, the hem of the towel at the top of my breasts. I stared at him in the mirror as he looked at me, the edge of his desire sharp. My pulse throbbed in response, and I clenched my thighs together. He looked up, dark eyes nearly all pupil. "You should get dressed, Merry."

"Or?"

His throat worked as he swallowed. "We need to discuss some things before there's an *or*."

"Alright."

Coltor left the bathroom, and I pulled on a simple tunic that was several sizes too big and more like a dress than a shirt. Comb in hand, I steeled myself with a deep breath before joining him on my sofa. He'd lit a fire, and the gathering of little carvings appeared to glow from their place on the hearth.

Much of the fatigue that I'd been feeling at the celebration had gone, replaced by an energized anxiety that I knew would leave me extra tired when it passed.

"May I?" he asked, reaching for my comb.

"Sure."

"Thanks. It will be easier to speak if I have something to keep my hands busy."

"Oh?" My cheeks heated, and he hadn't even started talking yet. "Is this about the mate thing?"

"Yes. What do you know? So that I know where to start."

Hailon and Lovette had both told me their own stories, how the mate bond had presented and what it meant to be fated to someone. There didn't seem to be any difference whether the bond belonged to a demon or a stone kin. Not to mention that Magnus and Grace were a pairing much like Coltor and I were. Could be. My heart fluttered an odd rhythm as I corrected myself. I relayed what I knew to Coltor as the strokes of the comb through my damp hair relaxed me.

"Yes. Did they mention what happens if one refuses a bond? Or ignores it?"

"No."

"Mmm." He was quiet for several moments as he finished combing through my curls and braided it into one long plait. When he was done, I turned to face him. He looked crestfallen.

"Why do you look so sad? How could you doubt that I feel a similar way for you as you do for me at this point? Did you miss that I was throwing myself at you in the bathroom?" I was teasing, but it was too heavy in the room to lighten things much.

"I don't doubt, and I didn't miss it. Trust me when I say I wish it were that simple."

"Make it simple. Explain why you're hesitating." I ran the backs of my fingers down the side of his face, and he took my wrist in his hand, kissing my knuckles.

"Do you have a burning behind your ribs, Merry? An ache that intensifies when I'm near you? When we touch?"

Regretful that he was dealing with such discomfort on my behalf, I shook my head. "Maybe a little, but not so much that I'm bothered. I'm sorry."

"Don't apologize. It's different for everyone and even if you're of witch heritage, you're human." His eyes went wide. "Please don't misunderstand me, Merry. I don't think any less of you because of that. It makes no difference to me who your ancestors were. I'm attracted to *you*. Whatever that means."

Everywhere our skin touched tingled, and I realized I had been having some odd sensations. "My heart beats irregularly now and then. Like it's jumped into my throat, all fluttery."

His mouth twitched into a grin. "I've gotten that too."

"Is that evidence of the bond?"

"Perhaps."

"You still haven't said what you're worried about."

"A bond is forever, Merry. This is not something to enter into lightly. Once we're intimate, the bond is sealed. There's no undoing it."

"Forever?" The word even tasted heavy. I thought of my mother, how she'd promised forever to my father, but he'd disappeared when they were both still young. She'd tried three more times after him, swearing it each time, but it had never worked that way, not even when they'd begun with enthusiastic love and the best of intentions. "What happens if it's ignored? What if we just keep on as we've been, or ... go our own way?" I had a visceral response to saying those words. My gut wrenched, and I broke out in a cold sweat.

"The pain will likely increase over time. Madness is a risk, worse the longer we live. Likely me more than you. But Merry"—he took my hands in his and met my eye, not looking away—"I would never ask you to make this kind of decision based on this risk. I would bear it, if that's your choice, without hesitation." I nodded, thoughts swirling, but I couldn't make my tongue work. "There are known cases where pairs refused a bond, and some have lived centuries before things got bad." He swallowed hard, like the flavor of that half-truth was bitter.

"I wouldn't want to cause you pain, Coltor. I can't imagine doing so willingly for months or years. Centuries would be outright torture."

He bowed his head and released my hands. "I should go. I have to do my patrol."

"Even with everyone here? And the ceremony?"

"Yes, the doorways don't sleep, and I need to get back on my routine." He got to his feet and leaned down to kiss my forehead. "Rest yourself, Merry. Decisions do not have to be made right now."

I disagreed. It was wholly unfair for me to continue things with him knowing what I did now if I didn't intend to see things through.

I stayed on the sofa until the logs in the fireplace had burned themselves out, exhausted but too wrapped up in considering the possibilities to sleep.

"WE AGE DIFFERENTLY."

"Greta can provide an elixir so your lifespans match," Hailon countered. "I took it. So did Calla and Greta herself of course. I'm not sure about Grace."

"You took it already?" I gasped. "How long will you live now?"

Hailon shrugged. "No idea. Might be hundreds of years. It doesn't really matter as long as neither of us have to face a lifetime or more without the other."

My heart squeezed. "That's actually so sweet, Hailon."

She blushed and shrugged, clearly amused but mildly uncomfortable. "Any other concerns?"

"What if something happens and we need to split up?" Again I was struck with the feeling that I might be sick just considering such a thing.

"Then you do what you need to do. There might be consequences, but you deal with them like everyone else."

"Everyone else doesn't have a magical bond that might hurt or kill them if it's broken."

Hailon yawned, thoroughly bored with my panicked debating. "Are you done?"

She'd arrived early to check on me, carrying party leftovers for breakfast, and then we'd gone to help with the cleanup. Jacks had gone back through the portal with Ophelia, and the stone kin were just as efficient in taking their equipment out as they had been bringing it in. The glade was set to rights and empty again before midday, and shockingly quiet now that most of the animals had moved on. We'd gone back to her cabin for some lunch, and we were still in her kitchen while I tried to talk out my messy thoughts.

I lowered my head against her dining table, my heart throbbing sorely. "What if he wants children, Hailon?" I peeked up at her. "After everything I went through with my mom and siblings ... that's not something I want for myself."

"You'll have to have that conversation with him." She reached across the table, covering my hand. "And I think you should, that's a big commitment either direction." She sighed and sat back in the seat. "Is there nothing positive you want to use in your considerations? Like the fact that he's ruggedly handsome? Tall? Has wings? Is a little scary?"

"The wings are very nice."

She brightened. "Jacks seems to like him."

"He does." His commentary about Coltor honestly weighed pretty heavily in my considerations.

"What about the fact that he's clearly obsessed with you? Has been since you first arrived."

"Hailon, don't be ridiculous." I laughed at her exaggeration.

"I'm not! I think he actually might be. It started with a carving a day but very quickly escalated to literally growling at people when they came to watch over you for a bit when you were unwell."

My heart skipped. "He did not."

"I was just trying to let him take a nap and get your hair washed, and he nearly bit my head off." She smirked, which told me she wasn't being entirely truthful, but I appreciated the push to remember the reasons I'd started falling for him. "You look yourself again, by the way."

"Thanks. I feel pretty much back to normal today." Which honestly felt like a massive accomplishment considering all that had happened.

And I had, I admitted to myself, thoroughly fallen for him. He was kind, attentive, and patient. We'd worked out our differences, and I felt I understood him, even when he turned inward and got frustrated. He didn't try to make me feel smaller in his presence; if anything, he allowed me to flourish while watching to be sure I was safe. He might have a vicious bark, but he handled me gently.

"I hate this."

"Love is truly the worst." Hailon's expression was dreadfully serious, at least until she burst out laughing. "Listen, you know I can relate. I was not looking for any kind of relationship, nor did I recognize what was happening between Seir and I for what it was as early as I should have. All I'm saying is, don't make a choice you'll regret out of fear of turning into your mother, Merry." My breath stalled. She'd somehow narrowed in on the crux of my hesitation. "You're not her, never were, never will be. You have all of us too. Me, Seir, Ophelia. Everyone at d'Arcan. You are not alone, and if you decide that Coltor is the one for you, you'll be even less so. You'll almost certainly be invited to join the stone kin clan. Whatever you decide, we're behind you. Remember that if the Fates chose him for you and you for him ... there's a reason. Lots of them."

There were, I knew that. We'd been over many of them several times.

Her words touched a place that had needed reassurance without me realizing. I tended to feel very alone—that came along with my independence. But I wasn't, and I had everything I needed to make my choice.

I just had to decide whether I was going to be a coward or fully embrace the life that the Fates had carved out for me here in the glade.

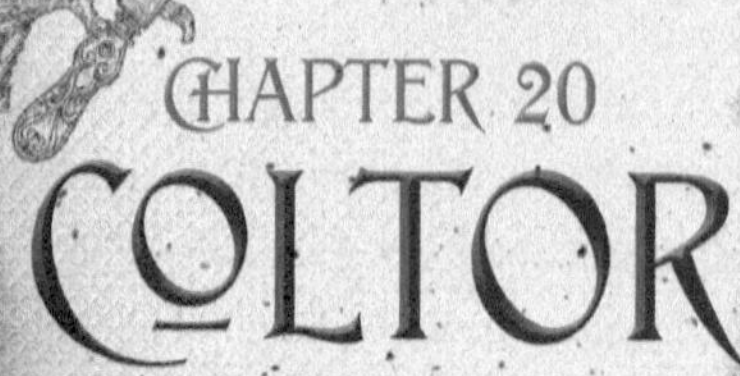

CHAPTER 20
COLTOR

I CAME BACK FROM my patrol to find Merry waiting for me on the little porch of my hut. My heart dropped into my boots as I tried to discern her blank expression. I'd spent all night twisted up in my thoughts, wondering what she'd concluded after my revelation. I felt like one massive, exposed nerve.

"Merry? Is everything alright? Feeling okay?"

Her voice was painfully neutral. "I'm fine. I brought dinner. More leftovers from the party. If they don't get eaten, they'll go bad."

"Okay. I could eat." I wasn't sure that was true, but I would try. "Did you rest?"

"A little."

I opened the door and gestured for her to go in before me, thankful I kept everything tidy. Plates were already made up and set for the two places. I went to the kitchen sink and washed up, trying to breathe through the anxious heartburn that had cropped up.

Once we were seated at the table and making a half-hearted attempt to eat in the heavy silence, Merry finally started talking.

"I have three siblings. For nearly their whole lives, I was as much a parent to them as our mother was to any of us. She married and divorced three times after my father went missing and struggled to function when things got stressful." She set her fork down, no longer even pretending to push things around on her plate. "Things were nearly always stressful." I nodded softly in empathy. "I raised her children while I still was one. Granted, I was a teenager by the time Mattias came along, but I was the adult and bore the weight of responsibility for us all." Her gaze met mine, and I hated the hesitation I saw there. "I don't want my own babies, Coltor. Not now, and likely not ever."

I stared back at her. Of all the directions for the conversation to go, this was not one I would have chosen. "That's … completely understandable. I think perhaps the Fates took that into consideration when they chose you to be Keeper, actually."

She frowned. "What?"

"Someone responsible for all of creature-kind probably won't have time to be chasing tiny humans around as well. So, it follows that your lack of desire to have your own children was part of the equation."

She started laughing, and it escalated quickly to the point she had tears running down her face. I worried they weren't only from amusement. "You rarely say anything I expect you to."

"Thank you?"

"Coltor, do you want children?" Her exasperation with me was plain in her tone.

"Not really. I'm not good with noise, and younglings are very loud. They're messy and unpredictable, and I imagine that if I find myself craving interaction with one there are plenty of children at the conclave I could talk to. Maybe one of my siblings will have a child and I can just be the strange uncle who lives in the ruins." She flopped against the back of the chair, mouth half open. "Did I say something wrong?"

She shook her head. "No. Not at all. I'm ... confused."

"About what?"

"I was quite sure that was going to be a significant problem."

I frowned. "Is that really such an issue for people?"

"Absolutely."

"Odd creatures, humans." I was only half serious, but it made her smile which brought me much joy.

"You want to be stuck with such an *odd creature* for eternity?"

My heart flipped in my chest. "I'd never be bored."

Merry stared at me again, and I finally relaxed, allowing the smile I'd been fighting to come out. "Have you been teasing me?" she asked.

"Only a little."

"I've been a wreck all day. Terrified. Nervous."

"Me too, Firebird. Are we through with all that now?"

"Yes, I think so."

"Good."

Anticipation built up around us as we stared at one another across the table. My senses were all tingling, my chest a hot ache. Merry was on her feet a split second before I was. She launched herself at me, arms winding around my waist and face pressed into my shoulder.

"I'm scared that something will happen and it will end and we'll both be badly hurt."

"I can't promise that isn't a possibility, but I can swear to try to be worthy of you every single day."

"Ugh, why are you so sweet?" She gazed up at me in a way that made me want to carry her off to my bed and keep her there forever. I leaned down slightly, and she pounced, crushing her mouth to mine, hands on my shoulders as she lifted herself up on her toes.

I groaned into her mouth, all the anxiety of the day melting away as our tongues tangled and she pressed her body against me.

"I'm not," I insisted, breaking away to take a few panted breaths.

I grabbed her ass in my hands and lifted, forcing her to lock her legs around my waist. "I will get overwhelmed," I warned, pressing her up against the wall. Her legs tightened around me, and she tilted her head back. The scent of her heavy in the air between us, I leaned in, licking a line up her throat before pressing an open-mouthed kiss over her pulse. "I will sometimes need space. I might lash out, but I will always apologize and mean it."

"Me too." She moaned out, making my blood roar as I nipped down on the tendon in her throat. "All those things." Her center ground against me, friction building through the cloth. "Animals will show up at terrible moments. I will be needed by others and have to sometimes choose my duty as Keeper over you." Merry's fingers were tugging at my shirt, trying to get it untucked from the waist of my pants.

"I'll have to do the same. I am at the mercy of my command. I could be sent to the training outpost for weeks at a time or be stationed somewhere else." The very notion made me feel like raging, but I didn't focus on it. I pulled my shirt off in one swipe, returning my mouth to hers as she wiggled against my grip. "There is no going back, Merry. You will be mine and only mine."

"Good. I don't share well either. At least, not anymore. I've been spoiled since I got here, I find I rather like having things all to myself."

I growled, the sentiment speaking to the more primal parts of me. "Too many clothes."

She squeaked as I spun us both and walked her to the bed. I set her down on the mattress, tugging at her leggings while she pulled off her tunic. I dropped to my knees, and she rose up on her elbows, the heat in her gaze making my cock throb behind the stays of my trousers. We both stopped, the only sound in the tiny hut our mutual panting.

"Speak now, Merry. Is this what you want? Me? Us? This bond?"

Her curls bobbed as she nodded. "Yes. I want you, Coltor. Please."

She didn't need to ask twice.

I ran my hands along her delectable thighs, then hooked them under her knees and tugged her to the very edge of the mattress. She was bare to me, already glistening with want and perfuming the air with her arousal. I rarely struggled with the need to shift, but the challenge in her eyes had me straining to hold back. My wings ached to come out, and my fangs had sharpened, prickling against my lips.

"Please," she whimpered, and that broke me.

I lifted her legs over my shoulders and dove in like the starved creature I was. I laved over her slit with my tongue, her gasps and moans rumbling through me. When I fastened my lips around her clit, Merry's hips rose off the bed. The bond was roaring behind my ribs, hot and angry. Pushing the discomfort away, I began to tease her with my finger.

"Coltor." She panted my name, chest heaving as I played, the ache in my cock nearly as bad as the one in my chest.

I alternated the strokes—fast, then slow, and added a second finger. The way her body responded, accepted me, pulsed against me, made me feel drunk. When I returned my attention to the sensitive little nub, she twitched. I reveled in the gift of surrender she was giving me and sucked hard, angling my fingers toward that soft spot that made her moan.

Merry detonated under me, her cries muffled by the crook of her elbow.

I ran the flat of my tongue over her several times as she gasped for breath, the flavor of her etched into my brain.

"I've needed that for weeks, Firebird."

She answered in a noise that wasn't quite a word, but I took the meaning well enough. I shucked my painfully tight trousers and stood, her eyes raking over me in approval, the flush in her cheeks and widening of her eyes stroking my confidence. As I was about to ask her to confirm her desire, she hooked my legs with her feet and pulled me forward.

"I need you," she said, the words heavy.

I closed my eyes and breathed slowly through my nose. The bond was agitated beyond measure, burning and pounding behind my ribs.

"Forever," I reminded her.

"I accept," she said, hands reaching for me.

The very last threads of my will broke, and I crawled over her lithe frame, bracing my body over hers. Merry, impatient, lifted her hips and rubbed against my straining cock.

"Merry." I'd meant it as an admonition, but instead it became a prayer.

I notched myself at her entrance and lowered my mouth to hers. She angled herself up, drawing me inside her heat as she moved. I gasped as the bond expanded beyond my flesh. Nerve endings sizzled, flames bathed my chest and gathered along my spine. Unable to contain it, my wings burst free, flaring wide as I held myself over Merry's body with one hand.

Worry raced through me, that I'd frightened her, that this was too much. But my mate was not afraid. She was smiling up at me, her heels digging into my lower back, urging me forward.

So, I gave her what she asked for.

Fire lit up my veins as we moved together, her face growing more and more flushed as she chased her pleasure. I helped her along, fingers slick between us as we both devolved into breath and sensation. My name danced off her tongue once again as she clenched and cried out. I closed my eyes and drove deep, following her right off the cliff as my release barreled through me.

I sank down to my forearms after my wings finally retracted and kissed her soft and slow. Her hands tangled in my hair and I palmed her ass, keeping her close as the world settled again.

I pressed my forehead to hers, the bond quiet in my chest, a cool breeze from her open window blowing across my back. "Okay, Merry?"

"Perfect. You?"

"You're everything, Little Firebird." I exhaled, a rogue auburn curl tickling my nose. "Come on. Let's get you cleaned up before you fall asleep."

She groaned but allowed me to pull her into the bathroom, where I washed every inch of her supple skin, carefully shampooed her glorious hair, and made sure one more time that she was thoroughly satisfied before carting her back to bed.

As she snuggled into my chest, I drifted, serene and content, the scent of her hair in my nose, and peace I could hardly believe I'd been gifted in my heart.

"I HAVE TO go run my patrol," I whispered, deeply regretting having to leave Merry alone in my bed. I'd fallen asleep for longer than I'd expected, and was already behind, but I wanted nothing more than to continue resting with her limbs wrapped around me.

"Okay. Be safe."

My cock jumped, at the sight of her all disheveled in my sheets, but I willed the need away. There was no time for distraction. "I will." I pressed a kiss to her cheek, and she cuddled further under the blankets.

Outside, the stars were bright in the sky and a breeze that warned winter was on its way whipped through the trees.

I sped through my checks, still thorough but anxious to get through my duties so I could return to her side.

It was dawn by the time I was finished. I returned to my hut as soon as I could, but she hadn't slept in like I hoped. There was a little note on the dining table, letting me know she'd gone back to her cabin for a proper cup of tea.

She smiled as I crossed her yard, rising from her seat on the top step of the porch. She was wrapped up in a blanket to protect from the cold, a steaming cup cradled in her hands.

"I'm glad you're here," she said, setting the cup on the railing.

"Yeah?"

"Yes. Though I don't see a carving in your hand. I was hoping for a little creature to add to my hearth. I rather like them."

"I was short on time, but I'm glad to hear that." Her casual flirting had my heart thumping like I was a youngling again, and her being tousled and sleepy was perhaps the most gorgeous way I'd seen her yet.

"Join me for breakfast?"

"I'd love to."

Merry smiled and stepped off the porch, beauty in motion.

I saw it then, my whole future in a single vision, the truth of it so powerful I held my breath. The early morning sunlight blazed behind her, curls wild and open arms lit up like wings.

THE KITCHEN AT d'Arcan was not in any way a small space, but there were so many people in it at the same time, navigating around one another had become like a dance.

Grace hadn't stopped smiling, which was incredible to me, as we'd already been working without a break for several hours, and she'd started preparing at least two days before.

"Thank you, girls," she said, addressing Sara and Jana, who were short enough they could duck through the crush of adult bodies with ease. Grace wiped her hands on her apron as she made a pass through the room, expert eyes taking everything in. "Please take the tin of sugar to Merry and then bring up another basket of clean towels. Lay them out flat on the closest student table, okay? Not the family table, we don't want to ruin the finish."

"Yes ma'am," they chimed.

Having heard my name, I turned to accept the large container. "Thank you, girls."

"Welcome, Miss Merry!" The two girls dashed out the door to the dining room.

I measured the sugar I needed into my pot of bubbling fruit and started to stir. We were making jam. Apple, berry, and even some pear. We'd started the day chopping and blanching squash, tomatoes, green beans. Everything we'd harvested from our gardens, plus some things Grace picked up in bulk at the market. After the jam was poured and we stopped for a bit to rest, we'd be going into pickles. Cucumbers, carrots. Green beans and asparagus. Calla, Greta, Hailon, and I had all followed Grace's expert instruction, and now there were jars all up and down the kitchen countertops and lining tables in the dining room.

"Be sure you don't spill on your hand. Boiling sugar makes a nasty burn," Grace warned as Calla started carefully transferring her spiced apple butter into jars.

"Thankfully we're in the best possible place for being treated." Calla's mouth was clenched as she focused, but her eyes sparkled with mirth.

"I'm nearly there on the preventive's elixir," Greta added, starting in on some of the stacks of washing.

"Preventive?" Hailon asked.

Greta grinned and winked at me. "Yes, Coltor came to me a while back asking about something that could be taken ahead of possible injury. Quite smart actually, but difficult to nail down a perfect recipe for. I've had to send off for several rare plants to experiment with." She grew thoughtful, gaze far away as she dried one of the large pots. "Would be nice to have some of those expensive items more closely at hand for my work."

"You need a poison garden," I offered.

"Poison garden?" Grace asked, scuttling back and forth, wiping jar rims and setting on the special lids.

"It would have to be secured somewhere none of the students— or children, or animals for that matter—can accidentally get into it."

"Wait, what on earth is a poison garden?" Grace repeated.

"Just what it sounds like," Hailon offered. "We never had one in Ravenglen, most everything we needed grew wild in the mountains, but I loved the idea of putting one in the backyard for the extra rare things I never got to play with." We shared a smile.

"Usually, it's a garden that's locked and walled," I told Grace. "Plants that are deadly in one way or another. Only those with special skills and knowledge should be allowed in."

"Well, tell the headmaster what you need. You already got him going on the vegetables and a small orchard, I can only imagine he'd adore the notion of such a dangerous addition."

"I've got a wish list," Greta nodded enthusiastically.

"Tell me when to come talk with him, and I'll do my best."

Grace pulled out snacks and tea once everything was jarred, and we sat around the family table talking and laughing. It was so lovely to be part of a circle of women like these.

It was a day full of joy, even if by the time we were done my feet were aching and my back sore. My heart was full to overflowing, like our pantries were going to be.

COLTOR AND SEIR had been waiting for us on the glade side of the portal.

"Where are all the jars?" Seir asked when we stepped through, our arms linked but empty.

"They have to sit a while to be sure they seal properly."

His shoulders sagged, expression positively crestfallen. "I was told there would be pickles."

"We'll bring our share in a few days." Hailon promised with a laugh as we all started down the path.

"What else did you make?" Coltor asked after kissing my temple, his fingers threaded through mine.

"Jam. Vegetables. Beans. So much," Hailon said.

"There were jars covering every counter in the kitchen and multiple tables in the dining room. No chance of getting ill from malnutrition or going hungry this winter," I corroborated.

"There *are* pickles, though," Hailon assured Seir. "Five different kinds."

Seir perked back up. "I'll try to be patient then."

We said our goodbyes at the split in the path, and Coltor pulled me under his arm as we headed toward my cabin. As we came around the bend and my cabin came into view, I gasped.

"What on earth?"

Coltor was grinning. "They got quite far today. I was worried you'd come back early and catch the workers hurrying to leave."

"What's happening? Why is there another cabin being built right near mine?" Several small woodland creatures chirped excitedly then scattered as we approached.

He took my hand in his, kissing my palm as he gazed down at me. It was impossible not to melt under a stare like that. He could make me believe I was the only thing in the world just by looking at me. It was dangerous. Addictive. I loved it.

"Let me show you."

We walked along the front, Coltor gesturing in illustration without ever letting go of my hand.

"The main room will be your office. Shelves all the way around for books, contracts, ledgers. Space for a desk, a sofa. The demons have agreed to continue on as your couriers, so you only need go to the crossroads when you like."

"Kind of them," I smiled.

"This will be a big window on the side. The glazer is working on the colored panes still."

"Colored panes?"

"Like Ophelia's, the one with the picture in it."

My breath stalled in my throat. "You ordered me a *stained-glass* window?"

"Yes. I chose a botanical design that suits you. I think you'll like it."

"Why?" My heart was in my throat imagining the cost, and his thoughtfulness was making me emotional. The two together had me spiraling in confusion. "Coltor, that must have cost a fortune! I can't afford—"

"Don't insult me, Firebird. I chose what I wanted to. There is no part of the cost that is in any way your responsibility, nor your concern."

"But—"

"Merry. No." He sighed, staring at me until I relented. "It seemed a fair price for the labor it will take. And you needed one. So, you'll have one."

"Needed one? For what?"

"Somewhere to greet the animals that will come. They always go to Ophelia's pretty colored window, so ..." He shrugged again, like this logic was obvious. We rounded the corner, and I could see that the rooms had been designed to sit at the front of the dwelling for a specific purpose. The whole back side of the cabin sat lower than the rest and currently had no roof. My chest squeezed as I puzzled out what it was for.

"A greenhouse?"

Coltor smiled and nodded. "For all your seedlings. You can raise even the trickiest plants, I'm told. The glazer is also working on the special panes for the roof and walls. And in a few weeks, they'll be back to build Jacks a shelter. I only need you to tell me where you'd like it."

"Coltor." I marveled at the nearly completed rooms, a barrage of emotions flooding through me. I fought against the reflex to think I didn't deserve such things, that surely this couldn't all be meant for me. "I don't even know what to say, this is incredible. How long have you been planning this?"

"Not that long. Though I will say the builders were all very pleased to have a reason to come back here to work. Took very little to convince them to take this project on." He grinned. "Finding a time when you'd be away long enough to make good progress so I could surprise you was the most challenging part."

"This is ... There are no words. Thank you." Tears prickled in my eyes.

"You're welcome, Firebird." He kissed my knuckles, a satisfied smile putting a twinkle in his eyes.

I stood on my toes and drew his face down to mine, reveling in the way his mouth immediately softened.

"Where are we spending our evening?" I asked. We rotated frequently, though lately he'd been spending more time at my cabin than I spent at his hut. I got the feeling he was beginning to separate himself from the little barrack, but having our own spaces worked for us. For now.

"Yours. After a day on your feet, we need the bigger tub. Or we could go to the pools."

"Oh saints, a hot bath sounds so nice. Maybe another night for the pools, I don't want to get chilled on the way back."

"Come on then. I think there might even be something left to eat." He tugged on my hand, pulling me close as we approached my porch.

My gaze caught on the fallow garden beds. They needed to be turned and replanted for spring soon. I could hardly believe all that had changed in the short time since I'd come to the glade.

Coltor gazed down at me from the porch, expression a perfectly serene mask of adoration and patience. I took his hand, knowing that he'd lead me into the cabin and feed me dinner. Then he'd run us a bath, wash my hair, and tease me without a shred of mercy while he got me clean and made sure I was nice and relaxed. Then he'd take me to my bed, or the sofa, or the kitchen table, and dirty me right back up—several times—before curling his body around mine and allowing me to sleep better than I ever had.

And there was not a thing about that I would change or complain about.

As I stared at him, my night playing out in my mind, I realized what I was feeling in that moment was incredibly complicated and also impossibly simple.

My cabin, the glade, the gargoyle in it—they were *home*. And I would forever be grateful to have found it.

What about Merry's trip to the stone kin conclave?
Get the bonus scene by visiting:

https://BookHip.com/ZXNCMXQ

What's next?

Book 4 of The Demon Princes Series,
The Demon's Domain for Tap's story!

Book 4 of The Gargoyle Knights Series,
Gargoyle's Gem for Imogen's story!

Want to be the first to hear breaking news and
other info from L.? Sign up for her newsletter!

http://bit.ly/ALANewsletter

You can also join her reader group to chat
with her and other readers!

https://bit.ly/LilysReaderLounge

Did you like *The Gargoyle's Glade*? Leave a review
on Amazon, Goodreads or Bookbub to share
your thoughts with other readers!

ACKNOWLEDGEMENTS

I hope you loved watching grumpy Coltor (I think of him as having Shrek vibes) and Merry (a covert Disney princess if there ever was one) figure themselves and their bond out! This one has a special piece of my heart, just like the glade itself. It's also technically a full-length novel instead of a novella, but it's the story it needed to be. This world continues to grow and surprise me in so many ways, I'm not sure I'll ever get tired of hanging out with these characters. <3

Always and forever, thank you to YOU dear reader. You're simply the best and I love that you're going on this journey with me. THANK YOU.

To my husband and Write or Dies—I wouldn't be me without you. Home is not a place. XOXO

And of course Meri, who didn't know she was lending her name and giant, kind heart to a character. I hope I did you justice and that you're pleased with this kind of surprise. <3

For Caroline, whose enthusiasm and helpful input during early readings is unparalleled. You are a priceless gem.

Blessings on Krista who manages my em dashes, ellipses, repeated words and billions of commas so kindly, there's a cabin waiting for you, I swear!

All the delicious treats for Jessica & Stephanie for always making the final product gorgeous. I couldn't do it without your help and I mean that.

Art credits all day every day to Nya @guardianofshadows and Holly @thehollyfox who continue to make me the most stunning character art and Mya @myas_sketchbook for creating my world map. I wish I could spend ten times as much on your incredible work.

And special credit to my new wrangler Kaitlyn, who reminds me I don't have to do everything myself. You're the cat's pajamas and I'm so happy I get to hang with you. <3

Note: This world is planned to be seven demon books plus six gargoyle novellas. I hope you stick with us!

For sneak peeks, discussion and other fun tidbits, make sure you're signed up for my newsletter, & join my reader group.

ABOUT THE AUTHOR

L. Alexander writes Paranormal and Fantasy romance with sweet & spicy cinnamon roll heroes, fated mates, monsters, magic and more. She guarantees a happily ever after no matter what and has a soft spot for broody anime characters.

www.authorlilyalexander.com

@lilyalexanderwrites on Instagram

Lily Alexander on Facebook, TikTok, BookBub and Goodreads

L. also writes Contemporary Romance under the name Lily Alexander.

www.ingramcontent.com/pod-product-compliance
Lightning Source LLC
Chambersburg PA
CBHW031045310726
48969CB00007B/2131